# moon white

# moon white

color me enchanted

melody carlson

All rights reserved. No part of this publication may be reproduced in any form without written permission from NavPress, P.O. Box 35001, Colorado Springs, CO 80935. www.navpress.com

TH1NK Books is an imprint of NavPress. TH1NK is a registered trademark of NavPress. Absence of ® in connection with marks of NavPress or other parties does not indicate an absence of registration of those marks.

ISBN 1-57683-951-6

Cover design by studiogearbox.com
Cover photo by Trinette Reed / PhotoDisc
Creative Team: Nicci Hubert, Arvid Wallen, Erin Healy, Darla Hightower, Kathy Guist

This is a work of fiction. The characters, incidents, and dialogues are products of the author's imagination and are not to be construed as real. Any resemblance to actual events or persons, living or dead, is entirely coincidental.

Published in association with the literary agency of Sara A. Fortenberry.

Carlson, Melody.
 Moon white : color me enchanted / Melody Carlson.
  p. cm. -- (Truecolors series ; bk. 11)
 Summary: When, at her stepmother's urging, Heather explores Wiccan spirituality, she not only becomes isolated from her Christian friends, she falls deeper and deeper into the occult and faces shocking betrayals and threats to her very life.
 ISBN 1-57683-951-6
 [1. Wiccans--Fiction. 2. Occultism--Fiction. 3. Spirituality--Fiction. 4. Stepfamilies--Fiction. 5. High schools--Fiction. 6. Schools--Fiction. 7. Christian life--Fiction.]
 I. Title.
PZ7.C216637Moo 2007
[Fic]--dc22

                          2006033180

Printed in the United States of America

1 2 3 4 5 6 7 8 9 10 / 10 09 08 07

## Other Books by Melody Carlson

*Bright Purple* (NavPress)

*Faded Denim* (NavPress)

*Bitter Rose* (NavPress)

*Blade Silver* (NavPress)

*Fool's Gold* (NavPress)

*Burnt Orange* (NavPress)

*Pitch Black* (NavPress)

*Torch Red* (NavPress)

*Deep Green* (NavPress)

*Dark Blue* (NavPress)

DIARY OF A TEENAGE GIRL series (Multnomah)

DEGREES series (Tyndale)

*Crystal Lies* (WaterBrook)

*Finding Alice* (WaterBrook)

*Three Days* (Baker)

*On This Day* (WaterBrook)

# one

"I AM NOT EVIL," I SAY QUIETLY, TRYING TO KEEP MY VOICE CALM FOR THE SAKE of those listening to what should have remained a private conversation. We're sitting in the cafeteria with about five hundred other kids at the moment, and I do not get why my *best* friend wants to go here right now.

"How can you say that, Heather?" she persists. *"You want to become a witch!"*

I try not to glare at her. "Come on, Lucy," I say in a light voice. "Don't show off your ignorance to everyone."

"You're calling *me* ignorant? You're the one who decided to become a witch."

"Lighten up," I tell her. "And quit going on about the witch stuff, okay?"

"Fine. What would you call it then?"

I smile at Chelsea Klein. She's sitting next to Lucy and actually seems fairly interested in the strange twist our conversation just took. "I simply mentioned that I'm reading a book about Wicca," I say to Lucy. "No big deal, okay? That does not mean I'm becoming a witch."

Chelsea nods. "Yeah, lighten up, Lucy."

Lucy turns and glares at Chelsea now. "So are you saying that

7

you think it's okay if Heather does become a witch?"

Chelsea just laughs.

"I'm serious," says Lucy. "I mean, you're a Christian too, Chelsea. At least I thought you were. Anyway, you used to go to youth group." Lucy frowns now, as if she's not sure what she's stepped into.

"What's your point?" asks Chelsea.

"My point is, do you think it's okay for Heather to be dabbling in witchcraft?"

"*Dabbling in witchcraft?*" I repeat. "Lucy, why are you making this into something that it's not?"

"Because I'm seriously worried about you, Heather." She shakes her head like she thinks I'm totally hopeless. "I mean, you spend a couple of weeks in the British Isles, you start letting your step-mom read her tarot cards to you, and then you start doing all these strange things."

"What strange things?" I ask.

"Well, how about this whole vegan thing?" Lucy rolls her eyes. "Like just a couple months ago, your favorite food was pepperoni pizza, and now you won't even touch a milkshake. What's up with that?"

"So now you want to tell me what I should and shouldn't eat?"

"That's not what I mean." She frowns and looks frustrated. "I've been trying to act like I'm cool with it, although I really don't get what your problem with dairy products is. I mean we're talking about milk, right?"

"I already tried to explain to you about how I'm concerned with the inhumane treatment of dairy cows, but you wouldn't even—"

"Whatever!" Lucy holds up her hands.

"You should be a little more tolerant, Lucy," says Chelsea.

"Yeah," agrees Kendall, pointing to her brown-bag lunch. "I

happen to be a vegetarian myself. And I've been thinking about converting over to vegan too. You have a problem with that, Lucy?"

"Maybe you want to make yourself captain of the food police," teases Chelsea between bites of chicken Caesar salad. "The CFP."

"I wasn't even talking about food to start with," Lucy protests. "I mean, seriously, I don't care what you guys eat. I think that was just Heather's little smoke screen. I *was* talking about *Wicca* and *witchcraft* and the disturbing fact that Heather is becoming a witch."

"And I told you that's not what's going on," I say, still trying to maintain some composure here. I just don't get why Lucy is acting like this. Why can't she just chill for once? Just because I go to church with her occasionally doesn't mean I believe the exact same things that she does. Can't she accept that? "For like the tenth time, reading about Wicca does *not* make me a witch."

"Look, Heather." Lucy sounds really irritated now. "Pastor Hamilton says if it *walks* like a duck and *talks* like a duck, you can be pretty sure that it's a duck. Okay?"

This actually makes me laugh. "Fine, Lucy," I tell her. "I can walk like a duck and I can talk like a duck, but that still does not make me a duck. *Okay?*"

Lucy looks slightly stumped now, and Chelsea and Kendall both applaud. "Well said," says Kendall.

"Thank you," I say, grinning over my little victory. But Lucy looks like she's about to explode, or maybe implode. And despite myself, I feel a little sorry for her. I wish I could make her understand. After all, she is my best friend. And she's always there for me when I need her. Or rather she used to be. Suddenly I'm not so sure. I wonder if it's possible to outgrow some friends. Maybe the time comes when you have to cut your losses and move on. Still, I really do like Lucy. We've been friends since seventh grade, back when my mom got sick and died. Lucy reached out to me when I felt totally lost and alone. And I really don't want to lose her friendship. Maybe I just need to help her understand that Wicca is no big deal. Still, I hadn't planned on having a conversation like this in public.

"Listen, Lucy." I use my most patient voice. "I think the problem is that you don't really understand what Wicca is and what it's not—"

"I know that it's witchcraft, Heather. And Pastor Hamilton taught a class about the occult last year, and Wicca was part of that, and I know that people who are into Wicca also worship Satan and practice magic and—"

"That's not true," I protest. "Wiccans don't even *believe* in Satan. How could we worship something we don't believe in?"

"So you do admit that you're a Wiccan then?" says Lucy with a triumphant look in her eye, like she's caught me in the act.

"Maybe I am," I tell her, ready to give up. Have it her way. What's the point?

She looks at Chelsea then Kendall. "See, I told you she's becoming a witch."

I just sigh and start packing up the remains of my barely touched lunch.

"Well, she's a nice witch," says Chelsea sympathetically.

"Hey, can you put a spell on Marcus Abrams for me?" teases Kendall. "Or maybe just whip me up some kind of love potion that I can sneak into his Snapple?"

"Yeah, right." Why do I even try? "You guys just really don't get it."

"Then explain it to us," says Kendall, leaning forward like she's really interested.

"I would," I tell her, glancing at Lucy, "if I could manage to get out a complete sentence without being interrupted."

"Fine," says Lucy. "Explain away. I'll keep my mouth shut."

I study her for a moment, still trying to figure out why she seems so angry at me. "Well," I begin slowly, "for one thing Wicca has a lot to do with nature and the seasons and the sun and the moon and the stars. It actually makes a lot of sense when you think about it. And it's about doing good, not evil, and it's a very ancient religion. It's been around for about 30,000 years—"

"How can anyone know that?" challenges Lucy. "There's no recorded history that far back."

"I don't know," I admit. "But I read that there have been archaeological findings related to Wicca that go back that far."

"I don't believe it," she snaps.

"Obviously," I say.

"You said you were going to keep your mouth shut," Kendall reminds Lucy.

Lucy stands up now, slinging a strap of her bag over her shoulder. "Well, sometimes we need to speak out. And as a Christian, I can't just sit here and listen to my best friend talk about some Satanic religion and how it's so great." She looks down at me, then sighs. "I just don't know how you got so off track, Heather. But I still love you and I'll be praying for you." Then she picks up her tray, turns away, and walks off. And, okay, I realize that it's just Lucy's immaturity speaking, combined with her inability to accept change, and I shouldn't even react to her, but I feel like I've just been slapped.

# two

As I go inside my house, it occurs to me that a lot has changed around here since Dad married Augustine last June. And I have to admit that most of the changes are for the better. Augustine is an artist, and not only did she bring some of her own paintings into our home, but she also brought along a pretty nice collection of items from her artist friends too. But before she hung anything on the walls, she did some repainting. At first I wasn't too sure about her color selections, like the pomegranate red in the kitchen or the deep purple in the hallway, but after she finished the painting and then carefully arranged the art, I could see how dramatic and interesting it made what would otherwise be a fairly white-bread house. She obviously knew just what she was doing. Still, it catches me by surprise sometimes. Like today. And I do wonder what my mother would say if she were here to see it. She was a firm believer in neutrals.

Out of old habit, I start to dump my coat and bag on the island in the kitchen, then stop myself, remembering how this aggravates Augustine. Having been single and childless for so many years, she has this somewhat obsessive tendency to keep everything in its place. It's like every room is supposed to be a work of art and she likes it to look just so. I mean, even the sofa throw pillows, which are beaded and not comfortable enough to actually rest your head upon, must be arranged in a certain way—asymmetrical with three on one end and two on the other and the colors have to be in a special order too. I've almost got it figured out. Well, except that she likes to change things.

"It's a seasonal thing," she explained to me last week. "In the same way that the leaves fall from a tree in the autumn or the buds bloom in the spring, I like the interior of a home to change as well." And for that reason, we now have a great big ceramic pot full of branches by our front door. Dad stubbed his toe on it a few times when he let Oliver (our cat) in and out, but he never complained once, not about any of this. I think he really does appreciate the color that Augustine brings into our lives, even if things aren't like they used to be. To be honest, it did get pretty sloppy around here after Mom died. At first I tried to keep it together, but Dad didn't seem to care one way or another, so eventually I just let it go. I wouldn't exactly call us slobs, but we were pretty relaxed in our housekeeping.

"Hey, Heather," says Augustine as she emerges from her studio just off the kitchen. The little room used to be my mom's office, back when Mom ran her accounting business from our home, before she got sick. But Augustine pretty much gutted the room, put all Mom's old stuff in the attic, and then had a bunch of floor-to-ceiling windows installed along the south wall. She says the light in there is perfect for painting now. And I have to admit that it was an amazing transformation.

"How's it going?" I say as I hang my bag and jacket on the metal hooks Augustine installed by the back door, along with a wooden bench and a shelf for dirty boots and shoes.

She kind of frowns as she wipes her hands on the tails of an oversized denim shirt that's smeared with paint. "Okay, I guess."

"Just okay?" I ask as I open the fridge.

"Well, I guess I'm feeling uninspired. I've been basically staring at a blank canvas all afternoon."

"Uh-huh." I take out a pitcher of green tea.

"I think it's the changing of the season or something. It's like I'm being blocked by some external forces, you know? Have you heard if there's a storm coming?"

I glance out the window as I pour my tea. "It's getting a little cloudy out there. But this *is* the Oregon coast. Anything could happen."

She sort of laughs. "Yeah, I'm still getting used to that. My head is sort of like a barometer. I get these sinus headaches when the weather starts to change."

I nod and take a sip. "That's too bad. Weather changes a lot around here."

"So I've noticed."

"Is there anything you can do about it? Take some decongestant or something?"

"Actually, it's kind of nice having a barometer in your head." She smiles. "It's like a warning, you know?"

"A warning?"

"Yeah, our bodies are like that, Heather. They're designed to keep us in touch with our surroundings and ultimately to protect us. The problem is, we just don't pay attention like we should. Like you get a gut feeling not to do something, but then you just ignore it and go ahead, then later on you wish you'd paid attention to your instinct."

"Yeah, I've done that before."

"It's just such a shame that we have all these great intuitions and psychic abilities, but most of us never even tap into them. Especially in the States."

Augustine has lived abroad almost as much as she's lived in America. She spent a lot of time in the British Isles as well as Spain, France, and Italy. I was pretty impressed with how cosmopolitan she was when I first met her. I guess I still am. So different from my life.

"You seem quiet today," she says as I place my empty glass in the dishwasher. "Everything okay?"

I shrug. "I guess."

She pulls out a metal stool and sits at the island just looking at me with that kind of intensity that Augustine is so good at, like she's getting ready to paint my portrait or something. "Come on, what's up? I know something's bugging you. Is it me?"

I pull out a stool across from her and sit down. "No, it's me."

"Why's that?"

"Or maybe it's Lucy." I frown, unsure if I want to spill anything. I mean, it's not like I think of Augustine as a parent. But it's not like I tell her everything. She might be young and pretty cool, but she *is* married to my dad.

She just nods without saying anything. "What's going on with Lucy?"

"Lucy thinks I'm becoming a witch."

Augustine laughs. *"What?"*

"Because I've been reading that book about Wicca."

She nods with a knowing expression. "Yes, I can understand how that would disturb a girl like Lucy."

"What do you mean?" I'm surprised to feel defensive of my friend. *A girl like Lucy . . .*

She seems to weigh her answer. "Well, I don't know Lucy that well, but I do like her. She actually has a very deep spirit. I sensed that the moment I met her. And she has a very good heart and I know she means well, but . . ."

"But what?"

"I think she may be sort of trapped."

"Uh-huh?" I nod, remembering how I've had this exact same feeling about Lucy, although I'm not sure why. "But what's trapping her?"

"I think she's gotten stuck in her parents' belief systems. Lucy hasn't really come to her own real spirituality yet. She's like a little girl who's trying on her mom's high heels and jewelry and makeup, sort of experimenting with religion. Do you know what I mean, Heather? Almost as if it's not really her own unique spiritual journey."

"Yeah, I can kind of see that."

"I'm sure Lucy *thinks* she has her own beliefs, but they haven't really been tested by real life yet. So she's just masquerading around in what she's been told."

"Do you think that's why she's so upset about me, I mean the whole Wicca thing?"

"I think it threatens her beliefs."

"So what should I do?"

Augustine just shrugs. "I don't know, Heather. But I suspect the answer is inside of you."

"It's not like I'm really that into Wicca. I mean, I suppose there are some things I like about it. But I could just stop—"

"No," Augustine says quickly. "You don't stop your own spiritual exploration just because it makes someone else uncomfortable. I don't know that much about Wicca myself. Of course, I know their philosophy is compatible to my own eclecticism and pagan beliefs, and I know that Wicca is harmless and not something to be frightened of."

"I wish Lucy could see it that way."

"Maybe you'll help her to broaden her perspective. I would think she'd respect you for taking your own spirituality seriously and not compromising your own values."

"Yeah, maybe so." Her words are actually encouraging. "Thanks, Augustine. That helps me see things a little more clearly."

"Anytime, sweetie." She looks over her shoulder, back toward her studio, and sighs. "Now, if you could just help me."

"You mean with your art."

"I desperately need some inspiration."

"Why don't you take a walk?" I suggest. "I mean, you're always saying how we need to celebrate the seasons. The leaves are starting to turn colors now. Why don't you go out there and enjoy them?"

She smiles and nods. "Yes. That's a perfect idea. I don't know why I didn't think of that myself."

I look at the clock. "I better get moving too."

"Dance today?"

"Yeah."

"Now that could inspire me as much as a walk. I love watching you dance, Heather."

"Thanks, but maybe you should save that for when the weather's crummy."

"I don't know . . ." she grins. "I can get pretty inspired by bad weather too." She's going for her coat now. "But I think you're right. A walk sounds perfect today."

I run upstairs to my room and quickly change into my tights and leotard, finally pulling on my pale pink legwarmers, then grabbing my shoe bag. Sometimes I wonder why I still take ballet. Oh, I enjoy the discipline of it, and it does keep me in shape for other forms of dance, but it's not like I'm under any big delusions that I'll someday be a great ballerina. I realize that even though I'm relatively good at dance, I just don't have the kind of drive and dedication that's required to take my skills to the next level. Who knows, maybe I'll quit after the Christmas recital—after I get to dance the role of the Sugar Plum Fairy in *The Nutcracker*. It's not a hundred percent sure yet, but Naomi, my dance teacher, all but promised me the part. I've been dreaming of doing it since I was six and Mom started me up in ballet, just a couple of years before she started getting sick. I just wish she could be here to see me do it. I know it would make her happy.

I'm still thinking about Mom as I get into what used to be her car. I was only thirteen when she died from breast cancer, and even though it would be three years before I'd be old enough to drive, I begged Dad not to sell her 1988 Volvo. I insisted that I wanted us to keep it and that I would take care of it and drive it when I turned sixteen. He tried to convince me that I could have a different car, that I wouldn't like this one by the time I was old enough to drive. He actually told me that "no self-respecting teenage girl would want to drive around a twenty-year-old brown Volvo." But I told him I would prove him wrong.

And, as it turned out, I did. I totally love this car. And when I drive it, it makes me feel closer to my mom. Sometimes I even think I catch a drift of her perfume, Calvin Klein Eternity (it mingles with the aroma of old leather and the faded pine-tree freshener that still hangs from the mirror), but it might just be my imagination. Still, it's a good feeling.

It was especially comforting to have this car after Augustine came into our lives last year. I'd just started to practice driving in it when Dad and she got engaged. And I got my license just a month before the wedding. I think this car was like my little, make that large, security blanket. And I relied on it a lot after Augustine moved in and started redecorating our entire house. I mean, I'm mostly cool with the changes she's made, but sometimes I look around and I can't see a single trace of my mom. And I guess that scares me.

# three

THE ECHELON DANCE STUDIO IS LOCATED IN AN OLD BOXLIKE BRICK BUILDING in the center of our sleepy downtown district. I've been coming here for ten years now, and sometimes this place seems like my home away from home. Naomi Lamb owns the whole three-story building. She rents the first floor as a restaurant, which has served everything from Mexican to Thai food and currently puts out a fairly respectable Italian menu. Naomi uses the second floor as her dance studio. It's a pretty cool place with its shiny hardwood floors and one long wall with nothing but mirrors and barres, and the opposite wall with nothing but windows that overlook Main Street. And the whole place smells pungent with floor polish and rosin, along with something else, something sort of musty and old but good, familiar.

As usual, I park in the back and go through the side door, which leads to a dark, narrow staircase. These stairs go on up to a seldom-used third floor and a few old and mostly vacant apartments that my dance friends and I used to pretend were haunted back when we were little and looking for some cheap thrills. When I reach the second floor, I hear the strains of piano music echoing down the hallway. It's the intermediate ballet class, the one I was in a couple years ago.

"Hi, Heather," calls Katy as she dashes out of the bathroom, still pushing one of her arms into her pale blue leotard. "Looks like you're running late too."

"It's not even four yet," I point out.

"Oh, I thought it was past four." She adjusts her twisted sleeve and pushes her arm the rest of the way through. "I was studying at the library and lost track of the time."

I smile to myself as we walk into the studio. Only someone as academic as Katy Morris could lose track of time while studying. I'm not sure if it's because both her parents are teachers or because she's a Chinese adoptee (I've heard that Asians are scholastically superior), but Katy really takes school seriously. In fact, dance for her is secondary to her studies. I never quite got that.

We sit down on the bench and begin putting on our toe shoes. Only three dancers are in the *en pointe* class this year, and Naomi keeps threatening to drop Rebekah Sanders if she doesn't start practicing more. But at least Rebekah is here early today. I can see her already going through warm-ups in the back room. I hurry to lace and tie my ribbons. "I'm going to warm up too," I tell Katy, who's still fumbling with her tangled ribbons.

"Hi, Heather," says Rebekah as she does a graceful leg stretch, arching her arm in a gentle curve. Sometimes I think Rebekah could be really good if she put some effort into her ballet. But I suppose I'm relieved that she doesn't try harder. That allows me to stay where I like it most—at the top of our class. I suppose if our little dance school had a prima donna this year, not that anyone would ever say anything as lame as that, it would have to be me. But I've worked long and hard to reach this position. And I guess I sort of enjoy the status.

"How's it going?" I ask Rebekah as I join her at the barre.

"Okay, I guess." She sighs and pushes a strand of hair from her eyes.

I'm never sure what to talk to this girl about, since she does homeschool and sews her own clothes and enters baking contests, and her life is so totally foreign to me. But I know she's older than me, and I have been curious about her plans following graduation. Or does she even have graduation? Like will her parents throw a party and hand her a diploma? Will she make a speech?

"Is this your last year of doing homeschool?" I ask.

"Yeah. I might actually get my diploma by Christmas if I finish my math in time."

"Will you go to college after that?"

Her eyebrows shoot up and she looks slightly disturbed. "Oh no. No, I don't think so." She switches legs and turns away from me.

"Oh." I switch legs too. "So what will you do then?"

She lets out another deep sigh as she bends over. "I don't really know."

"But you know you don't want to go to college?" Okay, it's obvious this girl doesn't want to talk about her future. Whatever. Maybe I should just shut up.

"It's just that I wouldn't want to go to college right away," she says slowly, as if she's carefully gauging her answer. "I just don't think I'm ready to leave home yet."

"Oh."

"Hey, you guys," says Katy as she joins us. "Did you see the new girl?"

"New girl?" I glance over Katy's shoulder.

"Yeah. She's going to be in our class. Naomi just introduced me to her. Her name is Elizabeth and she's really pretty."

I notice the clock on the wall. "Hey, it's a couple minutes past four," I announce. So we all go back into the main part of the studio, and I see that Naomi is talking to a slender blonde girl who's about my height. "Come meet Elizabeth Daniels," she calls out to us. Then, one by one, she introduces each of us, telling a bit about our dance background, ending with me. "And Heather has been with me since she was this high." Naomi holds her hand down low, then reaches up and pats me on the head. "She's come a long way in her dancing too. I'm very proud of her."

"Thanks!" I smile at Naomi. This is high praise, coming from our teacher. Naomi's always been careful not to elevate anyone's talent over another's. That's just one of the many things I respect about her.

"Elizabeth's family moved to Westport last week," Naomi continues. "She was born in Connecticut, but her dad's work relocated them up here from Southern California." She puts an arm around Elizabeth's shoulders. "I know all about her, because Elizabeth's mother is my best friend."

"Naomi is my godmother," says Elizabeth. "She's the reason I originally got interested in ballet. She sent me a pink tutu when I was about four. After that, I was hooked."

"And Elizabeth has been en pointe for nearly three years." Naomi winks at us. "And I happen to know she's a very accomplished ballerina. I think she'll fit right in with our class."

Naomi claps her hands and calls out some instructions to Sienna, our new piano player. Sienna only started working for Naomi this fall, and she seems like a real character and slightly out of place in the dance studio, but she never says much and she plays really well. I keep thinking I should talk to her and make her feel more welcome. Something about her dark eyes reminds me of my mom. They have this sort of intensity, like she's thinking some very important thoughts. But there's no time for socializing today because we're already beginning our regular practice routine.

I quickly learn that not only is Elizabeth *accomplished*, she's also extremely good. In fact, she's outstanding. Normally I take the lead in our class, and Katy and Rebekah work to keep up with me, but today it's all I can do to keep up with Elizabeth. This girl is going to keep me on my toes—literally!

I've actually broken into a serious sweat when it's only midway through practice. And I'm also getting more than a little worried. Elizabeth Daniels is way out of my league. I suspect she's been to some pretty advanced ballet schools. Consequently, I feel certain there's no chance that I'll get the part of the Sugar Plum Fairy this year. Not with Naomi's goddaughter in the ranks. Combine her talent with her looks, including that long, wavy blonde hair, and it's plain to see that I'm history. Crud, Elizabeth even *looks* like the Sugar Plum Fairy!

I tell myself not to be jealous and I try to refocus my energy into a perfect arabesque, holding it just a second too long, which makes me lose my balance. Oh well.

As soon as class ends, I grab up my stuff, excusing myself by saying that I need to get home quickly, and then I leave. Of course, it's not true. I can go home whenever I like. I just want out of there. I wipe my sweaty forehead with the back of my hand as I scurry down the stairwell. Okay, I'm probably obsessing over this sudden feeling of displacement. I just need to catch my breath and regain some perspective. I know I wasn't dancing my best today. For one thing, I was too uptight. My best dance always comes when I'm relaxed. But how can I relax next to someone like Elizabeth? Maybe I just need to give it time. I go through these mental aerobics as I drive home, trying to reason with myself, but as I pull into our driveway I feel crushed. Maybe I'll quit ballet altogether. I'm tempted to call

Lucy and pour out my problems, but then I remember that Lucy is mad at me.

"It's the equinox this weekend," I hear Augustine saying as I come in the back door. "I think we should throw a little celebration."

"Uh-huh," says my dad.

I can tell by the contented tone of Dad's voice that he and Augustine are probably in the middle of one of their kitchen embraces. I hate walking in on them when they're like this. I feel so intrusive, so out of place. It's like they should still be on their honeymoon or something. They certainly don't act like the parents of a teenager. But then I guess they're still technically newlyweds. Even so, sometimes I want to tell them to get a room. Oliver rubs himself against my legs and I lean down and scoop him up, scratching under his chin until he purrs happily. I guess we all need a little affection sometimes.

Still, it bugs me that I don't recall my dad ever hugging my mom like that in the kitchen, back when she was still with us. Oliver jumps down and starts picking at his kitty kibbles, and I just stand there in the laundry room feeling like this isn't even my house. Maybe I should just slip back out to the garage and pretend like I'm not here. But I can smell something cooking, and I suspect that Augustine is putting together some kind of dinner for us. Since cooking's not exactly her specialty, I should probably stick around.

Augustine is vegan too, but my dad is not. Although he's recently given up red meat as well as poultry, he still eats fish and eggs and dairy. And I must admit that sometimes, especially when he makes a grilled cheese sandwich, I consider giving up the vegan thing myself. And I suppose if I was to be perfectly honest, I'd have to admit that I probably only stick with it because it's helped me lose a few pounds and because Augustine is so happy to have two vegans in the house. Not that I don't care about animals. I really do. But, like Lucy so frequently points out, milk cows probably don't really suffer that much. Still, I'd feel like a failure if I gave it up after only a couple of months. I can do better than that.

I hear little giggles and that kind of quiet talk that warns me this is a private moment, so despite the aroma of dinner, I tiptoe back out the door, get into my car and drive north. I have no idea where I'm going, but this stretch of the road goes along the ocean and I usually find it soothing. I drive all the way to North Bay, a small coastal town about twenty minutes from Westport. Mom and I used to come here to get ice cream sometimes, but the old ice cream store was replaced by a cheesy tourist shop a few years ago, the kind of place that sells a little bit of everything and has lots of plastic junk lined up in its grimy windows. Still, I drive by just for old time's sake. But I'm surprised to see that the store has changed. It looks classier. The sign says The Crystal Dragon, and some of the glassware in the window looks interesting. I pull in front and park, unsure as to whether it will even be open since it's nearly six. But I notice someone walking inside, so I decide to check it out.

A bell tinkles on the door, and the first thing I notice is the smell. It's an interesting mix of scents, very herbal and floral, but also sort of mysterious. I like it.

"Hello," calls a woman from the back of the store.

"Hello," I call back, pausing to look at a shelf full of candles.

"Can I help you find anything?" she asks as she approaches me. She's wearing a long multicolored skirt, the kind that looks all wrinkly, with a loose-fitting velvet top that's the color of moss.

"I just noticed your store, and it looked interesting," I say as I pick up an orange candle and sniff it.

"That one is for success," she says, "strength and authority."

27

"Huh?" I turn and look at her.

She sort of laughs. "Oh, TMI, right?"

Okay, now I'm even more confused.

"TMI, as in *too much information*. You probably just liked the candle for its scent, right? And I go on and on about things you don't really care about."

"It does smell good."

"It's bergamot," she explains. "That's an herb that promotes things like creativity and luck."

"Oh."

"You see, these candles are specially designed with colors and scents that enhance your life. The line is called Magic Sense, and you picked out a good one."

"So if I buy this candle and burn it, I will be successful and lucky?" I say in a slightly skeptical tone.

She smiles. "If only life were that easy."

I nod. "But I do like the scent." I pick up a red one. "What's this one do?"

"That one's for passion and love."

I take a whiff but find the fragrance overwhelming.

"It's scented with saw palmetto berry. It's supposed to help you in the bedroom."

Reminded of the scene I left behind in the kitchen, I quickly set the candle back. "I'll pass."

She laughs.

"I got a book about Wicca when I was in Scotland last summer," I say as I look at a display of crystals. "I've only read a few chapters so far, but I think it has some information about things like herbs and stones."

"Yes. They are all part of the balance of life. It takes a little time to figure out how all the elements work together, but once you start to understand these things, your life will become more balanced as well."

I nod as I consider this. Balance would be nice. I feel like I've been slightly off balance for months now, ever since Dad remarried in fact, and today I feel like I'm slipping totally sideways. "So using these things can help you get some control of your life?" I ask her.

She nods. "In a manner of speaking, yes. Knowledge is power, and understanding the earth and its elements can be very empowering. I have something for you," she says, walking over to the counter. She picks up something that looks like a stack of cards, then shuffles it a bit and finally hands one to me. "Here."

"What is it?"

"Read it."

I look down at the card in my hand. It's pretty with its ornate borders and a crescent moon with some small purple flowers below it. There are also some symbols that mean nothing to me, but then I see the word at the bottom. "Heather?" I read.

"Yes." The woman nods. "But turn the card over, dear. Read the back. It's an oracle card, sort of a divining tool. I drew it just for you. It should have some words of wisdom that are meant for your life."

I turn the card over and read aloud. "Beauty and immortality belong to you. You will be protected and good luck will be your companion. But beware of isolation along the way. The lovely heather sometimes grows in lonely places, creating barriers between themselves and those who have brought them pain."

"There you go," says the woman in a satisfied tone.

"That's amazing," I say, looking up at her. "Do you know me or something?"

She just laughs. "Well, we haven't been officially introduced, but you do seem familiar."

"I mean do you know my name?"

She shakes her head and looks slightly confused as she reshuf-fles the deck of cards.

"My name is Heather," I tell her.

Her eyes widen. "Oh. Well, I guess I did pick the right card then."

I hand the card back to her.

"No, dear, I think you should keep it. It really was meant for you."

I nod. "Thanks."

"And my name is Willow."

"Really?" I say. "That's your real name?"

She smiles. "It's very real. But do you mean is that what my parents named me? No. It's the name I chose for myself. They named me Cindy." She laughs. "And for some reason Cindy just didn't seem very spiritual."

"My parents actually named me Heather," I say, instantly real-izing how dumb that must sound.

"Well, your parents must have had some good insights. And you seem like a very spiritual person to me." She leans forward now, studying me closely. "Do you keep a Book of Shadows, Heather?"

"A what?"

"Come, let me show you." She motions me over to a shelf on the wall that's full of books. "Let's see." Finally, she locates a stack of ornate-looking hardcover books. She picks up a purple one, and on the front in gilded letters are the words *Book of Shadows*. She hands it to me, but when I open the book I see its pages are empty. The quality of the paper is very nice, but it's blank.

"There's nothing here," I point out.

She laughs. "Of course."

"I, uh, I don't get it."

"It's a book *you* must write, Heather. It will be your own Book of Shadows."

"Oh."

"Sort of like a diary, but much more. It's a place to record personal thoughts, meditations, sketches, recipes . . . oh, whatever. But you don't let anyone else read it. Well, unless you really want to. It's very private, you see."

I stroke the smooth leather cover, temporarily blocking my vegan conscience as I run my fingers over the embossed letters. "I like that."

"I'll tell you what, Heather, since this is your first time in my shop, I'll give you a 20 percent discount for all purchases made today. How's that?"

"That's great," I say. I turn the book over to see that it's $20. The candle is $15. I'm not that great at math, but with 20 percent off, I'm guessing my total should be around $30. Willow shows me another book that she thinks will be helpful, as well as a few other less-expensive items, including some incense and herbs and stones. The focus of most of the items seems to be self-discovery and power. The total, even with my discount, comes to more than $50, which surprises me, but fortunately I have my debit card, which taps into a fair amount of savings thanks to a small life-insurance policy that Mom put in my name. Then Willow writes down some titles of other books that she recommends. "Just in case I'm not in the shop when you come back. I have a girl working here part-time, but she's really a novice."

"Thanks."

"And this is a good website," she says, handing me a small card.

"A friend of mine developed it. A lot of the websites aren't trustworthy. And some just operate so that they can make money by selling their junk. The items they sell aren't authentic, so you have to be careful or you can get into trouble."

"Thanks, Willow," I say as she hands me my bag. "I don't think it was a coincidence that I ran into you today."

She solemnly shakes her head. "No, I'm sure it wasn't. Come see me again, Heather."

It's just getting dusky as I drive back toward Westport. I pull out my cell and hit the speed dial for home. Hopefully they're not worried. But Augustine answers and sounds just fine. It does bother me a little that I lie to her. Instead of telling the truth, I say that I stayed in town to have coffee with a friend and lost track of the time. I don't even know why I do this, because I doubt that she cares one way or the other. Dad, on the other hand, wouldn't approve of me just taking off like that and driving out of town without telling anyone. He thinks my car's not totally reliable and that he should know where I am if I'm not within ten miles of home. Naturally, I think this is just typical parental paranoia. So as I close my phone I reason that some lies are acceptable, even good. Especially if they're meant to protect someone, like my dad.

# four

"WE'RE HAVING AN EQUINOX PARTY ON SATURDAY," SAYS AUGUSTINE AS SHE sets a piece of eggplant casserole on my plate.

"What's an equinox?" I ask as I spread some garlic hummus on a piece of flatbread.

"It's a very special time of year," she explains. "The day and night are the same length. It represents the changing of the seasons."

"Remember how Augustine and I were engaged on the vernal equinox?" my dad says as he sprinkles a heap of shredded parmesan cheese onto his chunk of casserole. It's all I can do not to grab the container and dump some on mine too, even if it does have milk. Augustine really tries to make healthy food, but sometimes it just doesn't taste quite right.

"Oh yeah," I say. "I remember how Augustine said it was a good sign that you asked her on the first day of spring."

"And then we got married during the summer solstice," Augustine says, winking at Dad. "We made sure the planets and stars were aligned properly and did this thing right."

"So Augustine thinks that the autumnal equinox would be a good time to have our friends over, a way for her to meet some people."

"You can invite your friends too," she says. "It's for all ages."

"Augustine already called Brandon Lichtner about the music."

"You're having live music?"

"Yes," says Augustine. "I'm hoping the weather will be nice enough to have a bonfire outside, and the band can play from the gazebo and we'll have dancing on the deck. I'll make a lot of hanging lanterns, out of old canning jars and twisted wire, and we'll put little tealights inside and hang them from the trees. It'll be beautiful."

"It does sound pretty."

"So you'll invite your friends?"

"I guess . . ." Okay, I'm not too sure what Lucy would think of something like this, especially since she's not too comfortable with Augustine anyway. But Kendall and Chelsea might like it.

"How was dance?" asks my dad as he pours himself a glass of wine, holding it up to the light to examine its clarity, which I'm thinking is a little murky. My dad makes his own wine, and some batches are better than others.

"It was okay, I guess." Then I decide to make my announcement. "But I was sort of thinking about quitting."

"Quitting?" Dad sets down his glass and frowns at me. "Why?"

"Oh, I don't know. I think I've sort of outgrown it."

"But you're *so* good," says Augustine. "You can't quit."

"And this is your year to be the Sugar Plum Fairy." Dad tosses me a hopeful smile.

"Maybe not."

"Maybe not?" Dad looks confused now. "Why not?"

So I tell them a little about the new girl. "She's Naomi's goddaughter, and she dances like she's been to some really good schools. Her family moved here from Southern California and—"

"Her last name isn't Daniels by any chance?" asks Dad.

"Yes," I say. "Elizabeth Daniels. Do you know her?"

"I don't know *her*, but I've had the pleasure of meeting her dad recently." His brow creases. "Anthony Daniels is the developer of the Yaquina Lake property."

"The development that your firm is fighting?" asks Augustine.

"That's the one."

"And his daughter is the one who's going to steal Heather's chance to dance the Sugar Plum Fairy?" Augustine looks seriously disturbed as she holds a knife in midair.

"Calm down," I say in a joking voice. "She's not stealing my chance. She's just better. And she's Naomi's best friend's daughter."

"This is all wrong," says Augustine. "You've been dancing for Naomi for years. You can't just let this interloper waltz in and take your—"

"Elizabeth isn't taking anything," I say.

Augustine nods and sets the knife back into the casserole. "Yes, I'm sure you're right. And I have to give you credit for handling this so maturely. I'm sure I'd have been mad with jealousy when I was your age."

I shrug. "Well, what's the point?"

"Even so," says Dad. "You can't quit. You can't even assume that the Daniels family will still be here by Christmastime. We're hoping they'll be so discouraged when they see our claim that Anthony Daniels will tuck tail and run."

"Really?"

"Yes. Let alone the wetlands laws, he has all sorts of hoops to jump through if he plans to make a resort out of Yaquina Lake."

"That's such a lovely lake," says Augustine. "I'd hate to see them spoil it."

"So would I," I admit. "Remember when we used to go canoeing on it, Dad?"

He nods. "Yep. And I can't bear to think of a schmaltzy golf course going around the west end of it."

"That would be a tragedy," I say. "I mean, that's where it goes off into the dunes and—"

"And golf courses waste so much water," says Augustine. "From what I've heard, this area's water supply is already hard-pressed."

"Well, Mr. Daniels has proposed a saltwater redemption plant to recycle the water for use on the golf course."

"Oh."

"And he has some big-shot attorney who's well versed in environmental issues—rather, in how to get around them."

"Well, I'm glad you're there to oppose this Daniels guy," says Augustine. "And I think Heather better stick with her ballet too."

Dad lifts up his wine glass again. "I agree. Here's to Heather, our favorite Sugar Plum Fairy."

"To Heather," says Augustine, holding up her glass.

"Do I get some wine for this toast?" I ask Dad as I hold up my glass of green tea.

He considers this. "Only if you promise not to give up your dancing."

I nod. "Okay, it's a deal."

Augustine hops up and gets another wine glass from the hutch behind the table, quickly pours a small amount, and hands it to me. Then we all toast. But I can't help but make a face after one sip, and then Dad laughs.

"I guess I should've warned you that the blackberry wine wasn't worth making a deal over," he says. "But a deal's a deal. No backing out of ballet, Heather."

"That's right," says Augustine.

"I'll do my best."

I offer to help Augustine clean up after dinner, but she informs me that it's Dad's turn to do KP and that it won't be fair if I help him. "We're still trying to figure out how to balance the household chores," she says. "Since I cooked dinner, he is supposed to clean up. Without help."

"Fine with me," I say. "I have homework anyway." Then I ask in what I hope is a nonchalant way if anyone called while I was gone. Okay, I'm wondering if Lucy called and wanted to apologize. But it seems no one called. So I thank Augustine for dinner, excuse myself, and go up to my room. But instead of going straight to homework, like I probably should do, I open the bag of things I bought at The Crystal Dragon. Taking them all out, one by one, I carefully examine them, then put them away. I light the orange candle and turn out the lights. I set the candle on the center of my dresser, where it's reflected off the mirror. For a moment I just stare at my own reflection in the flickering light. My long straight hair, which is normally the color of bittersweet chocolate, is tinted with mahogany henna. Augustine helped me to do that shortly before school started. And right now it looks redder than usual in the amber candlelight. My face in comparison to my dark hair looks extra pale and my cheekbones, which I get from my mom, seem to stand out more than usual in the shadowy light. I suppose in some ways I do look a little witchy. But not necessarily in a bad way. More like mysterious, mystical, enchanting perhaps.

I look down at the porcelain fairies that are also on my dresser. They look almost as if they're posed to begin some kind of ceremonial dance around the candle. I began collecting fairies years ago. My parents would get them for my birthdays, Christmas, Easter, and now I must have close to a hundred fairies in various forms throughout my room. I suppose I should've outgrown them, but for whatever reason, I haven't.

Maybe my love of fairies is related to my love of ballet, or maybe it's something else, but I've always admired the delicate grace and sweet beauty of woodland fairies, and when I was little I used to actually pretend that I was one of them. Wearing an old tutu and a set of homemade wings, I'd go flitting around my mom's flower garden, picking a few blooms and further decorating my costume. My mom even took some candid photos once. She used to keep one of them in an engraved silver frame by her bedside, although I have no idea where it is now.

The fairies seem to take on a new life in the flickering candlelight, and it's almost as if I can sense a newfound energy in myself as well. Maybe it really is a result of the combination of the color and scent in this candle, or maybe it's just my imagination, but oddly enough I feel like dancing. I'm still wearing my leotard and tights and, feeling strangely energized, I put on an old Enya CD, one I scavenged from my mom's music collection, and I begin to dance. I dance and dance and dance until my legs feel like wet noodles.

And then I flop down onto my bed and begin to write in my new Book of Shadows. I fill up three pages with writing, and to my surprise it's about my mom. It's *all* about my mom. I describe how much I loved her and how I miss her and I go into quite a lot of detail about how guilty I feel sometimes, especially when I think of all the things I could've done differently while she was alive. But more than anything else, I write about how I wish I could talk to her right now. I wonder what she would tell me, what direction she could give me about Lucy, about ballet, about Augustine and Dad, about everything. I might even want to ask her about Wicca. Mom and I never really talked about spiritual things. I know she prayed and even read an old family Bible sometimes, especially as the time of her death drew near. But she was never a churchgoer, and to my knowledge she wasn't a Christian. At least she never told me she was. If only she could speak to me now.

I finally close my Book of Shadows and let out a long sigh. Even though it was hard to write all that stuff down, I actually feel better. It's like a load has been lifted. Still, more than ever, I have this longing to communicate with my mother. But then I see my U.S. history book sitting on my computer desk, and I have a feeling if Mom could talk to me right now, she'd say, "Quit wasting time and do your homework."

So I blow out my inspiration candle, turn on the lights, change into my sweats, and hit the books. But as I'm researching online for a report on the Louisiana Purchase, I see a pop-up ad that says, "You can talk to the dead." Like a dummy, I click on it. Of course, I can tell it's a stupid rip-off to get some poor unsuspecting idiot (like me?) to fork over money to some scam artist who pretends he can connect me to my long-lost loved one. Yeah, right. Then, as long as I'm distracted, I check my e-mail, thinking maybe Lucy apologized that way. But there's nothing. Not even a piece of junk mail. It's like no one wants to talk to me. I consider writing a note to Lucy, saying that I won't hold her words against her.

But instead, I begin to wonder if there might be some legit website about communicating with the dead. I type in the address Willow gave me, and the heading of one particular link there catches my eye. "Eliminate the Middle Man—Talk to the Dead On Your Own." So I click it and am impressed with the no-nonsense approach of this site. Plus they're not trying to sell anything. It's like they simply want to give you the tools to do it yourself. So I print out their short list of guidelines and set it aside. First, I realize, I must finish my homework. I really do believe that's what Mom would say too.

But when I'm done, or mostly done, I pick up the printout and study it. The writer compares talking to the dead to making a phone call on a cell phone. If you're in an area with poor reception, you might not get through. Or if you're in the wrong building, you might be blocked. Or maybe you just have a crummy cell phone. In other words, if you take some time and care in contacting a loved one, you might actually connect. There seem to be three basic steps. (1) You have to be willing to make the call. (2) You have to be willing to listen. (3) You have to be willing to talk back. The article also says that it helps to have a significant item that belonged to the departed or to be in a place where the departed enjoyed being. I walk around my room in search of an item and finally stop at my jewelry box, taking out my mom's wedding ring—Dad gave it to me when I turned sixteen. I slip it onto my finger and then I think hard, trying to imagine one of Mom's favorite places. Our house has changed so much that I feel fairly sure it can't be inside the house. Then I remember how she loved the big old oak tree in the front yard. In fact, one year my dad considered cutting it down to let more light into the kitchen, but she begged him to leave it there.

So, wearing Mom's ring, I tiptoe down the stairs. It's quiet and dark down here, and I suspect that Dad and Augustine have turned in already. So I slip out the front door unnoticed, and I go out into the yard and stand under the big oak tree and look up. To my surprise there is a nearly full moon just emerging from the clouds in the east, and although the porch light is off, our entire yard and street is washed in a pale white light. The setting seems perfect. But now I'm trying to remember what I'm supposed to do. Oh yeah, just make the call. So I close my eyes and say, "Mom, are you there? Can you hear me? Do you want to talk to me?" Okay, I feel a little silly. But I also feel a little desperate. And how will I know if I don't give this a good try? I say the same thing several times, pleading with my mom to give me a sign, to show me that she's here, that she's okay, anything. But all I get is silence. That and a dog barking down the street. And the barking is really distracting. Plus I'm getting cold, and Oliver, who must've slipped out with me, is meowing to be let back into the house. And so I give up and go back inside.

I try not to feel too defeated as I get ready for bed. I mean, it's not like I'm an expert at these supernatural things yet. The important thing is that I'm starting to understand them, and I respect them, and I want to learn more. I remind myself how invigorating and empowering it felt to light that candle and dance to Enya tonight. And what a relief it was to write those things in my Book of Shadows. It's like something in me is coming alive — things are starting to make sense. And somehow I think the things that happened tonight have something to do with my mom. Somehow I think maybe she was watching me. But maybe there was something wrong with my connection or reception when I tried to make contact with her. Maybe I should try it again, perhaps in another location. Anyway, I don't plan on giving up. This is just the beginning.

# five

"HOW'S IT GOING?" LUCY ASKS ME THE NEXT MORNING. I CAN TELL BY HER crinkled brow that she's still worried about something. I'm guessing it's my spiritual welfare. But at least she's talking to me. That's something.

"Fine," I tell her as I close my locker.

She smiles and seems relieved. "Oh, good."

For some reason this reaction worries me. What is she assuming here? Does she think that just because I said *fine*, everything between us is peachy? Even if that was possible, I'm not sure that I'd like it. For one thing, I think she owes me an apology.

"I was really praying for you last night, Heather," she continues with bright eyes. "I was down on my knees just begging God to show you the truth, and praying that the truth would set you free."

"Really?" Now this actually surprises me because, as ironic as it seems, that's exactly how I felt. "Maybe your prayers were answered."

"Seriously?"

I nod cautiously. "Yeah. It felt like I was really freed up from something last night, Lucy. It was this amazing spiritual experience, like I'm on the brink of something that's going to be life changing, you know?"

"Oh, Heather, that's so cool."

"Yeah, it really was." Okay, even as I say this, I suspect we may be talking about two totally different things. And if Lucy knew exactly what I was doing last night, well, she'd probably freak.

"And I was thinking as I was praying, Heather, remember how Pastor Hamilton told you last year that you need to be baptized?"

I don't say anything. It's not like I haven't heard this before. The pastor nagged me for months to take the plunge into the dunk tank, and according to him, it must be done in front of the entire gaping congregation. He says it's so that I can "partake in the Lord's Supper," but I'm not sure what I think of all that. And the idea of standing down there in front of everyone, sopping wet and holding up my hands like I've seen others doing, some of them breaking down in uncontrollable sobs . . . well, it's pretty freaky. Consequently, I just haven't been able to make myself do it. I don't even think it's exactly necessary.

"So, anyway, I thought maybe that's your problem. You're being rebellious against God, Heather. And if you want your heart to be right with God, you need to surrender and be baptized by Pastor Hamilton. Does that make sense?"

I frown. "Maybe to you."

"Oh."

"Listen, Lucy, I don't want to hurt your feelings, but my spirituality is different than yours, okay? I need to explore some new things, and I need to figure it out on my own. I'm not like you. I can't just blindly accept some canned religion and—"

"It's *not* a canned religion." Lucy is giving me that look now. That look that tells me, once again, I have stepped over some invisible spiritual line. Like a lightning bolt might come down and zap me at any given moment. I almost expect her to step away from me just to protect herself.

"Okay, whatever you want to call it," I say firmly. "Your brand of religion just isn't what I need right now."

"So you're not giving up Wicca after all."

I let out a frustrated sigh. "How can I give up something that might actually work for me? I know you don't get it, but there are other forms of spiritual power in the universe. And for the first time ever, I feel like I'm finally on to some real answers, like I could finally get a grip on my life. Why would I want to give that up?"

She frowns and shakes her head now. "Then I won't be able to be your friend anymore."

"Just like that?"

"Yeah. I talked to Pastor Hamilton yesterday, and he made it perfectly clear that I'm not to spend any time with you, Heather." She looks at me with what appear to be actual tears in her eyes. "I really believed that you'd come around, especially last night when I was praying so fervently. But it looks like . . . like I was wrong."

I get ready to reason with her now. "But can't you see that I need—"

"No!" She holds up a hand like a stop sign. "I am totally serious about this, Heather. Witchcraft is an abomination to God. I cannot be around you if you're going to continue in it. That's it." And then she turns and walks away.

I press my lips tightly together and just watch her go. My best friend is ditching me because of my personal beliefs. Talk about spiritual persecution. Okay, the truth is I don't feel all that surprised by this. I mean, it was obviously just a matter of time before we parted ways. But here's the weird thing—I don't feel nearly as hurt as I thought I'd be. It's like I knew it was coming and now it's over with. I need to just let it go. And so I take in a deep breath and then slowly exhale. It feels sort of symbolic, like I'm blowing away my friendship with Lucy as I do this. As I walk toward the English department, it occurs to me that Lucy brought a lot of negativity into my life. I mean, her religion is so restrictive, it seems like it's mostly a list of don'ts. I honestly think I'll be healthier without her around. Sure, it might be lonely, but just the same, it's time to move on.

"Hey, Heather!" calls a girl's voice from behind me. I turn to see that it's Elizabeth Daniels and she's hurrying to catch up with me. It's funny seeing her here at school. She looks so ordinary wearing a pair of torn jeans and a light blue T-shirt. Who would guess she's a talented ballerina? "I thought that was you," she says as she joins me. "What's up?"

"Not much," I say, forcing a smile. "How's it going?"

She rolls her eyes. "I'm still feeling kinda lost. I mean, this school is way smaller than where I used to go, but not knowing anyone is a real bummer. So who do you ask for directions?"

"Well, you know me," I tell her. "What are you trying to find?"

So she tells me and I point the way.

"Uh, Heather," she says in a tentative tone. "Do you, uh, do you usually eat lunch with a certain group of friends?"

"Yeah, sure." Then I realize what she's really asking. "Do you want to join us?"

Her blue eyes light up when she smiles. "Oh, could I? Lunchtime is by far the hardest part of the day. I feel so conspicuous sitting by myself. And then if someone tries to be nice to me, well, I'm just not sure what their motives are. But at least I kinda know you. I mean, we do have ballet in common."

"Yeah," I say. "Okay, why don't you meet me by the north entrance to the commons, and we can go in together." I almost mention that there will be room since I have one good friend who will not be joining us today, but I'm not quite ready to divulge that much. Besides, there's the chance that Lucy could freeze me out of our little group. It's possible that Chelsea and Kendall will take her side, although I doubt it. Anyway, I know it can't hurt to be nice to Elizabeth. After all, she's Naomi's godchild.

As I walk toward the English department, I suddenly remember what my dad said about her dad last night. And I feel sort of irked and I wonder whether I really want to befriend this girl. I mean, isn't she the enemy? Then I realize that it's not her fault her dad's a jerk. Unless she thinks like he does, I should probably at least give her a chance.

Mr. Finney is talking about symbolism in Creative Writing this week. And today's assignment is to find a graphic symbol and write about its meaning. Okay, it seems a pretty vague assignment, but Mr. Finney isn't exactly known for his clarity. The poor guy looks older than dirt, but I think he retires this year, which in my opinion is about a year too late. Anyway, I saw some symbols in the book I got from Willow yesterday, and perhaps that's why I stuck it in my backpack. I pull it out and quickly discover a pentagram. To me it simply looks like a star, a five-sided star like I learned to draw when I was little. But I find that each point of the star has a meaning. The top represents spirit. Going clockwise, the next four points represent water, fire, earth, and air. It seems simple enough. I also learn that the shape of the star is mathematically perfect, although I have to admit these formulas go right over my head (which is mathematically imperfect). But it seems that the pentagram is related to the human form as well, meaning that our head plus two hands and two feet make up five points. And apparently this is all symbolic of energy and balance and some other things. And when you put a circle around the star, you make the energy infinite—in other words, magical. I attempt to draw a five-pointed star but immediately realize that it's not perfectly balanced. I try again and again and finally realize I will probably need a ruler and compass to get it right. And then class is over.

I'm still thinking about pentagrams when I spot Elizabeth waiting for me by the commons. She smiles and waves and seems genuinely pleased to see me. It's funny how it takes so little to make some people happy. Unfortunately, this is not the case with Lucy. I spy her as Elizabeth and I walk into the cafeteria together. And I can tell Lucy is watching us. Her face is a mixture of curiosity and something else. Could it be jealousy? Well, I tell myself I don't care. It was Lucy's choice to end our friendship.

I see Kendall and Chelsea already at a table, and I decide to take advantage of the situation by taking Elizabeth over for introductions. Then Elizabeth and I leave our bags with them and go over to pick out some lunch. Now if Lucy wants to join them, she will have to join us as well.

"Is that all you're having?" asks Elizabeth as I get in line to pay for my food.

I look down at my regular green salad and whole-wheat roll with no butter and just nod.

"You're not anorexic are you?"

I laugh. "No. I'm vegan."

"Seriously?"

I glance at her cheeseburger and fries and try not to feel food envy. "Yep."

"Wow, how do you have enough energy to dance when that's all you eat?"

I just shrug, then hand the cashier some money.

"I always thought one of the cool things about dancing was that you could eat all you want as long as you dance it off. But I wouldn't last twenty minutes on what you're eating, Heather."

I try not to think about this as I go to sit down. Naomi pointed this same thing out to me not long ago, after I told her about becoming vegan during the summer. She said that dancing required protein for muscle tone and endurance and that I wouldn't last long as a ballerina on a total veggie diet. I hoped to prove her wrong. Now I'm beginning to wonder.

"Where's Lucy?" asks Kendall as I lift my fork.

I shrug and take a bite.

"I saw her a few minutes ago," says Chelsea.

"Oh, there she is," says Kendall, pointing over my left shoulder.

"Why's she sitting by herself?" asks Chelsea.

"Who's Lucy?" asks Elizabeth.

"Haven't you met her?" asks Kendall.

"No," I say quickly. "And if you must know, Lucy isn't talking to me."

Kendall's eyebrows shoot up. "Is she still mad at you for being a witch?"

I sort of laugh. "Yeah, something like that."

"You're a witch?" asks Elizabeth.

"No." I let out an exasperated sigh. "I'm just learning about Wicca. And Lucy thinks that's really evil, and now she won't have anything to do with me."

"Seriously?" says Chelsea. "She told you that?"

"Well, you heard her yesterday," I remind them. "And today she pretty much read me the riot act. Like it's her way or the highway."

"Lucy can be fairly stubborn," Kendall explains to Elizabeth.

"She's really religious and she takes everything in the Bible totally literally."

"Whereas Kendall here is only mildly religious," teases Chelsea. "And she doesn't even read the Bible."

"I do too, sometimes," protests Kendall. "I just don't get as involved with it as Lucy does. She's one of those people who go to church every time the doors are open, and she prays about everything."

"Lucy means well," I say in defense of my old friend. "But she's just stuck following her parents' example. Instead of thinking for herself and taking her own spiritual journey, she's just letting them tell her which way to go."

"Wow, that's pretty profound," says Kendall.

I don't admit that it was my stepmom who came up with that.

"Lucy looks lonely," says Chelsea. "Should I go ask her to come join us?"

"It's up to you," I say. "I have no problem with her joining us. She's alienated herself."

But no one gets up to invite Lucy to come eat with us. And I have to admit that part of me is glad. Maybe Lucy needs to see what it feels like to be excluded, since that seems like what she's doing to me. Chelsea and Kendall ask Elizabeth about why she moved to Westport and where she's from and just general things like that, and it's interesting hearing her answers.

"Well, I might as well get it out into the open," she says. "My dad is the notorious developer of Yaquina Lake."

It gets quiet at the table now.

"Really?" says Kendall, leaning forward.

"Yeah, I probably should've kept my mouth shut, huh?"

"Maybe," agrees Chelsea. "I mean, no offense, but my mom

would like to have your dad shot and his head mounted as a hunt-ing trophy."

"Chelsea's mom is a real bird freak," says Kendall. "She wants everything that faintly resembles a wetland preserved forever."

"She's president of the local Audubon society," says Chelsea.

"And while we're confessing about our parental connections," I begin, feeling a little sheepish, "my dad's law firm represents the case against your dad's development."

"That's your dad?" Elizabeth looks at me in astonishment.

"I'm surprised Naomi didn't mention it," I say.

"Naomi doesn't like to mix politics with dance or friendship," says Elizabeth.

I nod. "Yeah, that sounds about right."

"And, just for the record, Naomi and my dad do *not* get along at all. And Naomi is totally opposed to the Yaquina Lake development."

"Wow, that must be hard," I say. "I mean, since your mom and Naomi are such good friends."

She nods as she picks up a fry. "Yep. And it makes matters worse that my mom was the one who originally got the idea to develop a resort up here. She thought it would be cool to live in Oregon."

"So are your mom and Naomi still friends?"

"Like I said, they just don't discuss certain things." Elizabeth dips a fry in ketchup. "Although, in all fairness to my mom, she's not too excited about the development now."

"Why?" asks Kendall.

"She hadn't realized all the ecological issues involved. I think she'd back down if my dad hadn't already invested so much into it."

"And where do you stand?" asks Kendall, which takes the

pressure off me, since I was wondering the exact same thing myself.

"I wasn't too sure at first. I mean, I'm used to all the nuts who are opposed to any kind of development. My dad goes through this stuff all the time, and if the extreme environmentalists had their way, I'm sure we'd all be living in tents and eating grass for lunch. But then I saw Yaquina Lake last weekend, and, well, I'm not so sure now. It's really a pretty spot."

"Very interesting," says Kendall with a twinkle in her eye. "I see the making of a TV movie in this."

"Maybe you can sway your dad to change his mind," says Chelsea.

Elizabeth just shrugs. "I doubt it. That man is like a bulldog when he sets his mind on something. Besides, like I said, I'm still not totally sure where I stand. I've seen the plans for the development, and it's very thoughtfully laid out. It could really improve the local economy. And from what I've seen around here, that might not be a bad thing. I mean, you guys don't even have a cultural arts center."

Well, there's no arguing that this town could use a little boost to its economy, but even so! I am sincerely glad when it's time to go to class. To be honest, this is a conversation that I'd just as soon not participate in. I'm afraid I might get overly emotional when it comes to defending Yaquina Lake. It gets me thinking of how much my mom loved it and how we used to canoe there, not to mention its natural peace and beauty. Well, I'd hate to see it all ruined for the sake of the almighty dollar.

# six

"SEE YOU AT DANCE CLASS," CALLS ELIZABETH ON THURSDAY AFTERNOON. We're both getting into our cars in the school parking lot. Hers is a fairly new silver Acura, which I'm guessing wasn't cheap and looks like a million bucks next to my old Volvo. Not that I care. My car has charm and class and is my last remaining connection to my mom. Still, there's an undeniable contrast.

Liz (as she's asked me to call her) and I have been hanging together for two days now, and I think she actually considers me a good friend. Not to suggest I don't see her as a good friend as well, but I suppose I'm holding her at arm's distance. I'm not even sure why. Maybe I'm just being cautious. For one thing, there's her dad's development plan, which made the newspaper again today, combined with the fact that my dad will be opposing him in court next month. Besides that, she's my competition in ballet. Put those two issues aside and I think our friendship might work out.

Not that I should be too picky right now, since Lucy is still giving me a serious cold shoulder along with the silent treatment. And today she beat me to the cafeteria and planted herself with Chelsea and Kendall, somehow getting a couple of our other "lesser" friends to fill in the other seats so that there wasn't room for Liz and me to join them. But Liz and I were like "whatever" and went off and sat by ourselves. The funny thing is that as soon as we did this, a couple of guys came over to our table and began talking to us. In fact, they were a couple of very cool guys.

I tried not to act too surprised when Hudson Schwartz and Porter Brannigan came over and started to chat. I introduced them to Liz, and they sat with us for a while. We didn't really talk about anything specific, mostly just joked about the crummy food and how we wished it was still summer. Then they said, "See ya," and left. I wanted to peek over to see if Lucy was watching. She and I have both had a crush on Hudson for years, although I've always laid special claim to him since he and I have the same initials as well as the exact same number of letters in our last names. This fact doesn't escape me now. Nor does it escape me that Hudson is cuter than ever with his dark curly hair and big brown eyes.

As I drive toward home, I'm suddenly reminded of Augustine's reminder, just this morning, telling me to be sure and invite some of my friends to the equinox party. I'm not sure I'd have the nerve to invite Hudson, although I wish I did. But maybe Liz would. As I pull up to my house, I decide that I'll mention the party to her today at ballet. I'll ask her if she wants to come and maybe even hint that we could invite Hudson and Porter. Just for fun.

I've been doing "centering" exercises every day after school. It's a ritual that involves music, candles, incense, balance, and motion. It's kind of like dance, but more from the center of your being. It's a way to energize your spirit and empower you. And it gets me in the mood to practice ballet, which I've committed myself to do for at least two hours a day. I do my centering down in the basement, which is basically my own private space to practice ballet. My mom and I cleaned it out when I was about ten, installing a six-foot practice barre along with three full-length mirrors and some overhead lights. It smells a little musty down there, but if I light scented candles and incense, it's not too bad.

Since today is a dance-class day, I realize I'll only have time to do my centering exercises, but I'm hoping this will help me to dance better. I'm hoping that Tuesday was a fluke. Maybe Liz was just having an exceptional day or trying to show off because she's new. And maybe I was having an off day and allowing her to intimidate me. Now that I know her better, I think the intimidation factor has pretty much worn off.

"Ballet?" asks Augustine as I emerge from the basement with my shoe bag.

"Yeah. I gotta go."

"Did you invite anyone to the party?"

"I'm going to," I say quickly. "Do you think it's okay if I invite Liz?" I've already explained to her about how Liz isn't completely sold out on her dad's development and how I've decided to befriend her.

"I think that's a wonderful gesture," says Augustine. "And I, for one, would like to meet her."

"I just hope Dad doesn't initiate any confrontational conversations."

"Oh, honey, Vince wouldn't do that."

"Well, you make sure to warn him not to, and I'll invite Liz."

She smiles. "Anyone else?"

"I'm thinking about it."

"Good. Because so far I only have about fifteen people committed to coming. I'd really like to see about twice that here."

"I'll do what I can."

As I drive downtown, I practice some of the deep-breathing techniques I read about on the website that Willow recommended. I want to be centered and relaxed at class today. I want to do my best. I also want to go back to The Crystal Dragon for some more things. In fact, if I didn't have ballet, I'd go right now. But I remind myself not to get distracted. First things first. In fact, that's one of the things I really appreciate about Wicca—the sense of discipline and order that it values. I'm beginning to understand how the universe shows us that there is a correct way to do things and that life goes better if you don't fight it. It's better to embrace the energy and get the power to go with you. Then you can accomplish anything. That's what I tell myself as I park next to Liz's sleek Acura. I grab my bag and, holding my head high, hurry up the stairs to the studio. I know I can do this. I know I will dance my best today—and I think my best might be better than Liz's.

As we're stretching in the warm-up room, I start to tell Liz about the equinox party. But then I realize it might not be polite to bring this up with Katy and Rebekah listening. Not that I *wouldn't* want to invite these girls, but I suppose I don't really *want* to invite them either. It would just be too weird.

"What?" asks Liz as she executes a deep plié.

"Later," I say as I do a quick series of battement, grand. I smile, giving her a quick sideways glance meant to suggest this is private. She nods as if she understands, and no one is the wiser. Then we hear Naomi calling us into the main part of the studio, clapping her hands and instructing Sienna in French to play a slow number to start with. And as we begin to go through a routine, I feel stronger than ever, and my movements are clean and graceful. I try not to watch Liz, but I think I might be upstaging her, just a bit. And when the routine is over, Naomi claps her hands and compliments me on my jeté.

"Very nicely done, Heather." Then she starts us in another

routine. "Allegro!" she says, which means "brisk and fast." The tempo increases and suddenly I feel myself struggling to keep up. It's like I can't catch my breath, and finally, about midway through, I double over and clutch my aching side.

"Are you okay?" asks Naomi, coming over to me.

"I think so," I tell her. "I just got a cramp."

"Go get a drink of water," she tells me, "and then walk it out."

I go down the hallway to the bathroom, hearing the lilting tones of the piano continuing and the occasional thump of hard toe shoe against the wood floor. I feel like a failure as I stare at my image in the bathroom mirror. My face looks paler than usual and my skin has a taut appearance, but that may be due to the tightness of my ponytail. I remove the band and let it fall free. Then, holding my hair back with my hands, I stick my head down into the stained porcelain sink and get a drink directly from the spigot, taking long, cool gulps and ignoring the fact that the water tastes stagnant and rusty.

"Everything all right in here?" asks an unfamiliar female voice.

I look up with water still dripping from my chin and see Sienna standing in the doorway. "Naomi asked me to check on you," she explains. "She's showing the other girls a new step right now."

"I'm okay," I say, pulling my hair back into a looser ponytail. "Just tired I guess."

She's leaning against the doorjamb and adjusting the gold chain on her necklace with a slightly disinterested expression. Maybe she's just enjoying a break from the piano, and this makes me wonder if she likes her job. She rarely smiles. But once again those dark eyes remind me of my mother, and I find myself staring at her. Then she returns my gaze and I feel self-conscious.

"Is that a crystal?" I say in an effort to distract. I nod toward the pale purple stone pendant hanging from the chain.

Her eyes light up just slightly, and her lips almost curve in a smile. "Yes. It's a quartz crystal. It has good energy."

I sort of laugh. "Maybe I should get some of that myself."

She scowls at me now. "You shouldn't make fun of things you don't understand, Heather."

I'm sort of surprised that she even knows my name. "I wasn't making fun of it," I say quickly. "Seriously, I'm really into all that." I begin telling her about my visit to The Crystal Dragon and about some of the stones and herbs I purchased there and how I'm convinced that these elements are making a difference in my life.

"I just thought I'd do better today," I finally admit. "I've really tried to focus myself, and I did some exercises right before class. But it didn't seem to help much."

She nods as if she understands. "Something might be blocking your power. And if you're new at this, it's likely that you're doing some things wrong. Most novices don't get it right at the beginning. But if you ever want some tips, feel free to ask me. I've been practicing for years. I've even written a book."

"Really?" I try not to look too surprised. I mean, I don't like to judge people by exteriors, but Sienna, although somewhat bohemian-looking, is also sort of frumpy and pretty overweight and, if you ask me, not exactly the picture-perfect image of successful life—nothing I'd aspire to anyway. Not to mention her illustrious career of playing second-rate piano for a small-town dance studio. Not exactly impressive. Naturally, I don't say this. And yet, despite her general lackluster appearance, I'm still pulled in by her eyes. They're so similar to my mother's that it's like I almost feel Mom's looking at me now.

"I know what you're thinking," she says, catching me by surprise.

"But you need to understand I've gone through some hard times just recently. Just because I've practiced for a long time doesn't mean my life is perfectly on track."

I blink, then nod. "Yeah, I'm sure. And thanks for the offer of help. I'll keep it in mind. I'm sure I could use some pointers."

She nods. "Naomi is renting me apartment number three upstairs, if you ever want to talk or anything. And I should also tell you that I'm very experienced in communicating with the other side. That's what my book was mostly about. Just in case you're ever interested in anything like that." Then she gives me this long sort of perceptive look, like she knows way more than she's saying, and I actually get goose bumps.

Okay, my first reaction is to feel freaked, but I guess I'm also impressed. I mean, not only has this woman nearly read my mind, but I have a feeling that she knows I've been trying to speak to my mom recently. But instead of admitting any of this, I just thank her again and tell her that I need to get back to class now.

"Are you okay, Heather?" asks Naomi when I come back.

"Yes." I nod and join the line of girls. "Just a cramp. It's gone now."

We continue through our instruction without further ado, but I know that I'm seriously lagging. It's as if my body is rebelling against my mind, like my limbs refuse to cooperate. Even Rebekah and Katy are outdancing me today. I'm totally discouraged and consider making a mad dash out of here again when it's over—and never coming back. Too much humiliation.

"Heather," calls Naomi as we finish our last routine.

I can tell by her expression that she wants to have a private chat with me. I slowly walk over, careful to maintain my posture lest she tweak me on that too. "Yes?"

She crooks her long forefinger at me. "Come into my office for a minute, please."

So I follow her into the tiny cubicle that serves as her office, and she closes the door and leans against her desk. But even when Naomi leans, her spine remains straight. Good posture is essential to ballet. "You know that I don't like to interfere in my girls' personal lives, but I'm very concerned about you."

"Why?" Suddenly I think she may have heard about my involvement, albeit minor, with Wicca. I know that Naomi regularly attends a church, although she's not nearly as vocal about her Christianity as Lucy or her family. Still, she may disapprove of what I'm doing. And so I prepare myself for a spiritual lecture.

"It's this whole vegan thing," she says in a tired voice. "I just don't think it's the proper diet for a dancer, and I don't think it's helping you at all."

"Oh."

"And it worries me that you could develop a serious health problem. I just don't want to have you—"

"I was thinking about quitting," I say, eager to end this unsettling conversation.

"Quitting?" She blinks in surprise now. "You're giving up dance?"

"No, no. I was thinking about giving up being vegan. I've had second thoughts about it too. I don't really think it's working for me."

She actually reaches over and hugs me now. "Well, that's good to hear. Oh, I'm so relieved. I didn't want to say anything, but I've noticed a real lack of energy in you since you started eating that way. It concerned me."

I nod. "Yeah. I think I mostly did it initially because of my stepmom. We were in Ireland at the time and I sort of got into it. Augustine's been vegan for years, and it seems to agree with her and she says it keeps the weight off. But, besides that, I do feel bad for the inhumane treatment of farm animals. In fact, I may never be able to eat beef again." I sigh, considering this. "Anyway, I do think I'm done with being a vegan."

She grins. "Good for you."

"Although it's going to be kind of embarrassing to admit to everyone that I was wrong about this."

"It's better to admit that you've taken a wrong turn, then get back on the right road, than to simply wander around lost."

I sort of laugh. "I guess so."

For some reason, I feel a huge sense of relief now. I thank Naomi for her little intervention, then go back out to find Liz is dressed and waiting for me. "Did you want to talk about something?" she asks.

"Oh yeah." I sit down and untie the ribbons on my toe shoes.

"How about getting coffee?" she asks.

"Sure, want to meet at the WC?"

"The what?" she looks confused now.

I chuckle. "Westport Coffee," I explain. "We call it the WC."

"Oh." She laughs. "I thought you meant the water closet. You know that's like a toilet in England."

"Yeah, I know. And sometimes their coffee tastes like they got it from there too. But I usually get Chai tea anyway."

"Me too," she says with enthusiasm. "I love Chai."

So we agree to meet down there. The next class is lining up now, and the piano music starts in again. As I leave the studio, Sienna actually smiles and nods at me, and I wonder if I should take her up on that offer. I have a feeling there's more to that woman than meets the eye. I walk across the street and into the WC, deciding that today I'll have real milk in my Chai tea. No more soy glop for this girl! I step up to the counter and order my tea, then go over to where Liz is already seated at table by the window.

"My stepmom is planning this party for Saturday night," I begin. "You see, she's an artist and she's really into celebrating seasonal things, and anyway it's the autumnal equinox this weekend and Augustine wanted to have a party, and she wanted me to invite some friends, and I wondered if you'd want to come."

"Won't that be kinda weird?" Liz asks as the girl sets my Chai tea on the table.

"Well, yeah," I admit. "It's pretty weird. But then my stepmom is sort of a different—"

"No, I mean *weird* since our dads are sort of at odds with each other?"

I shrug. "I think it'll be okay. Augustine promised to ride herd on my dad. And he's usually a pretty agreeable dude. Besides, by the time he has a couple glasses of his homemade wine, he'll be a happy camper anyway."

"Homemade wine?"

So I explain about Dad's little hobby. "He might even let you sneak a taste, if no one's looking."

"Sounds like this could be fun."

I try not to roll my eyes. "Well, anyway, I'm sure it'll be different. Oh yeah, Augustine hired a band, and there will dancing. But it's hard to say what the food will be like since she's kind of a health nut. Still, the decorations should be cool—she's really a good artist."

"I think it sounds interesting."

"Right," I say. "Interesting. It should be."

"Did you invite any other friends?"

"Actually, I had this crazy idea today. You know when Hudson and Porter were talking to us? I thought about inviting them. Is that totally lame?"

"I think it'd be fun. You *should* invite them. They seem nice."

I kind of shrug. "Yeah, but they might not want to come. I mean it's kind of weird when you think it's a party mostly for grown-ups. But Augustine really wanted me to invite people too. I don't know."

"How about if I invite them?" she suggests. "I could say it's because I'm the new girl and I want to get to know some kids. Would that help?"

"Sure," I say. "That'd be cool."

"Then if they say no, you don't have to take it as a personal rejection. You can just figure it's because they don't like me."

"Yeah, right." I look at the pretty blonde girl sitting across from me. What guy wouldn't like her?

# seven

"I INVITED SOMEONE TO YOUR PARTY," I TELL AUGUSTINE AS THE THREE OF us sit down to dinner. It's pasta tonight, my dad's specialty with two sauces, one red sauce that's vegan-friendly and a white sauce with cream and butter. I go for the white sauce.

"Hey, what're you doing?" asks Dad as he notices my choice.

"Eating," I say.

Augustine frowns at me. "What's up, Heather?"

So I explain my recent dietary decision, even explaining how Naomi was concerned for my health and how I nearly collapsed at class today.

"Well, we can't have that," says Dad with a satisfied grin.

"You have to do what's best for you," agrees Augustine, but she looks disappointed.

"Who did you invite to the party?" asks Dad.

"Well . . ." I consider how to put this, glancing at Augustine for moral support now. "I invited Liz Daniels."

Dad just nods. "That's nice."

"You're okay with that?"

He sort of laughs. "Hey, I'm not a beast, Heather. Augustine already told me you might invite her. Nothing wrong with that. Who knows, maybe we can win her over and she can help convince her old man that —"

"No politicking at my party," warns Augustine.

"Sure, sure." Dad winks at me. "Wouldn't dream of it."

The next morning I change my outfit about six times before I decide on my favorite jeans and an olive green sweater that Augustine bought for me in Ireland. She says it brings out the color of my eyes. I also think it brings out the shape of my figure. Truth: The reason I'm taking such care has to do with Hudson. I can't stop thinking about this guy, and I'm hoping that he'll talk to me again today and that either Liz or I will get up the nerve to invite him and Porter to the party tomorrow.

At lunchtime, Liz and I meet at the door to the commons, and it seems she already has a plan in place. "We should get a table to ourselves again today," she says as we go into the cafeteria. "I think the chances of Hudson and Porter talking to us will increase if we don't sit with the other girls."

"Why's that?" I ask as I pick up a food tray.

"I think most guys are intimidated by a big bunch of girls."

I nod. "That makes sense."

Since Lucy is already sitting with Chelsea and Kendall again, we have the perfect excuse to go elsewhere. And it's a nice touch when Kendall tosses me a sympathetic look, like she's helpless to do anything with stubborn Lucy. I think she and Chelsea might even miss our company. Well, good!

Liz and I are nearly finished with our lunch and about ready to give up on seeing the guys when Porter and Hudson pop over and start joking around with us again.

"You girls going to the big game tonight?" asks Porter in a sarcastic tone. Everyone knows our football team will be toast after Bay View finishes with us.

"I don't know if I can bear to see it," I say.

"Yeah, it's going to be brutal," says Hudson.

"Why?" asks Liz.

So Porter explains the sorry state of our football team. "And it didn't help that all the good players graduated last year."

"They should've just cancelled the season," teases Hudson.

"Why don't you guys play?" asks Liz. "You look like you might be able to throw a ball and run."

Hudson just laughs. "No thanks!"

"We're into soccer," says Porter.

"I love soccer," says Liz.

"Me too," I admit. And that's the truth. "I'd rather watch soccer than football any day."

"Why don't you come watch us on Saturday then?" asks Hudson.

Okay, I'm thinking here's an opportunity. "Well, I would but I have to help my stepmom with this big party she's having on Saturday night."

"Our game will be over by four," says Porter. "The big party doesn't start before that, does it?"

"Actually, it starts at seven," I say.

"Hey, you guys should come," says Liz.

They look surprised now.

"Sure," I say. "If you want. My stepmom told me to invite anyone I want."

"Her dad is serving homemade wine," adds Liz.

I softly punch her in the arm. "Hey, you're not supposed to tell people that."

"Count me in," says Porter.

"I'll come on one condition," adds Hudson, "You girls have to come to our soccer game." Then he tells us when and where and we agree.

"See ya," calls Porter as they take off.

"Well, that was easy," says Liz as we stand and pick up our trays.

I try not to look too stunned. "Yeah."

"Want me to drive us to the soccer match tomorrow?"

"Ashamed to be seen in my car?" I ask, pretending offense.

"No, not at all. I like your car."

I nod. "Yeah, it has class."

"I'd drive an older one myself," she says as she dumps her trash, "but my dad's all into safety standards, so I'm stuck."

I laugh. "Yeah, you look really stuck."

After school, I leave quickly. I feel sort of bad for not waiting for Liz, but it's not like I promised her anything. Still, I'm barely driving down the highway when my cell phone rings. Now, my dad has made it perfectly clear that I'm not supposed to talk and drive, but thinking it could be Hudson, I answer anyway.

"Hey, why'd you take off so fast?" asks Liz.

"Huh?" I say as I try not to drive too close to the shoulder.

"I was looking for you at school, and then I go out to the parking lot and your car's not even there. Something wrong?"

"No," I say quickly. "I'm just running an errand. I have to go to North Bay."

"Oh, something for the party?"

"Yeah." Okay, that's partially true.

"Well, I wanted to ask you if you wanted to come over to my house tonight. I thought we could hang out there. Maybe you'd want to spend the night. My parents flew to Seattle this morning and I'm on my own."

"That sounds cool," I say. "Can I call you when I get back?"

"Yeah, sure."

Now I really had hoped to have time to myself tonight. Especially since I'm on something of a mission. My plan is to get some special ingredients that will help me with my life — particularly where Hudson is concerned. I also want to get something to help me with ballet. And this isn't something I really care to share with Liz. Maybe I can just make up an excuse not to go over tonight. Or maybe I can take care of everything before I go to her house.

To my disappointment, Willow isn't at The Crystal Dragon today. It seems she's at some big convention or something. Consequently, a girl named Jamie tries to help me, but I can tell that she doesn't know much more than I do about these things. In fact, she may know even less. She actually tries to convince me that lavender is for energy.

"No way," I tell her. "I know for sure that lavender is a relaxing herb. My stepmom uses it all the time in her bath as a calming thing."

"Sorry," she finally says. "I guess I should be reading up on this stuff more. But this job only pays minimum wage, you know, and I have a life."

"That's okay," I say, trying to read from a book as I pick some things out. "I'll figure it out myself." I'm not too sure about that "I have a life" comment. Like does she think I don't? Whatever.

After about thirty minutes, I think I have what I need. And, remembering something I read, I make sure that Jamie keeps my two formulas separate. I want them to be as powerful as possible.

Then I go home. To my relief, Augustine isn't around. I suspect she's getting stuff together for the party. I see that she's already made her little hanging lanterns, which are actually pretty cool. So I head up to my room to get some more things, then I take everything down to the basement, close the door, and light some candles and incense and put on some music. I read the section in the book about rituals, and first I go through a cleansing ritual for all my things and myself. Then I light the new red candle, symbolic of love, and I set it on the green altar cloth, also good for love. Using my just-cleansed ritual bowl, I combine the herbs and stones that will help to ignite love. And I invoke the spirit of Venus and repeat several lines of my own creation. Magic, it seems, is a combination of both old and new, and creativity is welcome. I do several other things, and when I finish, I feel both tired and energized. It's hard to explain. I wrap up the herbs and stones in a special cloth bag and stash this in my purse. Then I go through a similar routine, only with different ingredients, focused on my dance. Then I pour these herbs and stones into a different cloth bag and stash this in my shoe bag.

I realize it's nearly six o'clock and I still haven't called Liz back. So I blow out the candles and carefully place all my ritual tools into what used to be my toy box. I think I'll have to paint it sometime, maybe put some symbols on it that will help protect the power contained within it. Then I go upstairs, where I find a note from Augustine saying that she's meeting Dad for dinner and I'm on my own. No big surprise, since Friday is usually their "date night." So I call Liz and apologize for taking so long.

"I was about to give up on you," she says. "I tried your cell and got your voicemail. Is everything okay?"

"Yeah, of course. Everything's great. I just had a lot to do."

"Do you want to come over?"

"Sure." She gives me directions, and I leave a note and take off.

Liz's house is on the bluff that overlooks the ocean, and I'm guessing it's worth at least a million. Of course, they're just renting for now. "If we stay here, we'll probably build," she tells me after a quick tour of the impressive home. "My mom doesn't like this kitchen anyway. Have you had dinner yet?"

"Nope."

"Well, I could fix us something or we could go into town."

I shrug. "Whichever."

She gets a sly smile now. "I was thinking if we went into town, well, we might see someone . . . you know, like run into a couple of guys we both sort of like."

I nod. "Yeah, that could happen."

"If not, we could at least get something to eat."

"And if we didn't care about watching the hometown team getting its clock cleaned, we could stop by the football game."

She grins. "Yep, that's sort of what I was thinking too."

So we get into her car and head for town. We stop at Jack Hammer's, the local burger dive, and order some dinner. Not really ready for beef just yet, I stick with the fish sandwich and fries.

"It's so good not being vegan anymore," I admit as I take a big bite of my fish sandwich. "Eating out could be a real challenge around here."

"I'll bet." She nods as she picks up her burger. "And your energy should be coming back to you too."

"Yeah." Of course, I'm also thinking of the energy potion in my shoe bag. "It should."

"And before long you'll probably be dancing the shoes right off me."

I force a laugh. "Oh, I doubt that."

"No really, you're good, Heather." She looks serious now. "But I think your stamina was definitely lagging."

"I know. I'm glad that Naomi gave me a piece of her mind."

"And she doesn't do that too often, either."

"Not even with your mom?" I ask. "I mean, since they're such good friends?"

"They talk, but I can tell that Naomi keeps a lot of opinions to herself. I guess that's for the best."

"Yeah."

"I'm surprised at how much I'm starting to like it here in Westport," she says. "I wish we'd come here under different circumstances. Did you see the letters to the editor today?"

I shake my head as I sip my drink.

"Well, let's just say I'm glad my parents were already on their way to the airport when the paper came. It was pretty sad."

"That's too bad."

"Yeah, I hate it when debates gets all heated and emotional. People can say and do some pretty mean things. My dad is having this big meeting with the chamber next week, but I'll bet there will be protesters. It'll probably turn into a local media circus."

I just shrug. "Not much you can do about that."

"No. I just wish it would hurry and get over with."

I want to ask her which way she wishes it would go, but I have a feeling she's still uncertain. And I suppose, since I'm starting to appreciate her friendship, well, maybe I don't really want to know if she's supporting the development. Maybe ignorance really is bliss in certain situations.

We see a few kids from school at Jack Hammer's, but not the ones we'd hoped to "run into." So we head on over to the game. The score already looks dismal and it's only the second quarter.

"There they are," says Liz in a quiet voice, nodding down toward the front of the student section.

I reach into my purse and give the little white bag a squeeze, then actually slip it out and into my coat pocket. What can it hurt? I'm careful to keep my thoughts focused on Hudson, though. No way do I want this to backfire and attract the wrong guy. I suppose I feel just a little bit silly. But I shove those doubts away. I know they only invite bad energy. Instead, I smile and think about how cool it will be when Hudson realizes that he's madly in love with me!

"Let's sit up here," says Liz, pointing to an empty bleacher.

"So far away from them?"

She nods and sits. "Yes, make them come to us. Play hard to get, you know."

"Oh. Yeah."

And after about three minutes, just like magic, the two guys spot us and wave, then wander on up and sit down. To my delight, Hudson sits next to me, and Porter sits next to Liz. I didn't want to admit it, not even to myself, but my greatest fear was that Hudson might be interested in Liz. And, while Porter is okay, it's Hudson that I've set my heart on.

"What a cruddy game," says Hudson, rubbing his hands together to keep them warm. "We were actually thinking about leaving just now."

"We just got here," I say. "We almost didn't come, but town was pretty dead and we didn't have anything more exciting going on."

He laughs. "Yeah, Westport isn't exactly the hotbed of excitement."

"Are you guys still coming to our game?" asks Porter.

"Sure," says Liz. "You guys still coming to Heather's party?"

"It's a deal," says Hudson, smiling at me.

I give my little white bag a squeeze and smile back at him. I can't believe what's happening just now. I mean, only a week ago, my life seemed pretty pathetic and painfully boring, and suddenly everything's changing. Just like magic!

# eight

LATER THAT NIGHT, LIZ AND I DECIDE WE'LL DRESS UP FOR THE PARTY. WELL, not too dressy. But Liz's closet is like a miniature boutique and, lucky for me, we both wear about the same size in both clothes and shoes. So she insists on picking out an outfit for me, deciding on a soft red-and-black rayon skirt that's got some "kick" in it and a clingy black top, complete with black strappy high-heeled sandals that I'm guessing cost a bundle.

"You look totally hot," she says as I stand in front of the mirror.

"And this will be fun to dance in too," I say as I give a little twirl. "You think we can get those boys to dance?"

"We're dancers, aren't we?"

I laugh. Then she holds up several things to choose from for herself. We finally decide on the purple outfit and gold shoes. "Purple looks more autumnal than the pink," I tell her. "Augustine will appreciate that."

Then we stay up late watching a new DVD and talking about boys. Liz has already had a couple of fairly serious boyfriends, and she's surprised when I admit that I haven't.

"Why not?" she asks.

I consider this. "I'm not sure. I guess it might have something to do with Lucy."

She frowns. "Lucy? What? Is she gay or something?"

I laugh. "No, but her parents are really conservative, and she's only allowed to date boys from her church, and then only if it's with a group."

"Pretty limiting." Liz pops a chip into her mouth.

"Yeah. And since Lucy wasn't dating, well, I guess it was easier for me not to date either."

"Looks like times, they are a-changing."

We decide not to stay up too late, since we both want to make sure we get enough beauty sleep to look our best tomorrow. Then, after a quick breakfast in the morning, I tell Liz that I better go home and see if Augustine needs a hand before it's time to go to the soccer game.

"I'll pick you up a little before two," she says.

When I get home, I help Augustine by hanging her little glass lanterns in the trees outside. Then we start putting out the tables and chairs that she rented. She wants them arranged in groups of four and eight. "This is looking good out here," I call out to her from across the yard.

"And the weather is promising," she calls back. "This might turn out all right."

As we hang strings of little white lights around the deck, I imagine Hudson and me dancing here tonight. Then Augustine and I put more lights around the gazebo where the band will play.

"I think that about does it for out here," says Augustine, proudly looking around at her efforts. "It should look dreamy by tonight."

"Liz is going to be here to pick me up in a few minutes," I tell her. "Mind if I get ready now?"

"Not at all. Thanks for the help, sweetie."

"I can't wait to see how it all looks tonight," I say as I head into the house. "I think it's going to be a magical evening."

I hurry to my room and quickly change into shorts and a sweatshirt. The weather is really warm today, and since I still have some summer tan left on my legs, I think, *Why not show it off?* I'm just putting my hair into a fresh ponytail when I hear Augustine calling my name.

"Liz is here," she says.

I hurry downstairs in time to see Liz admiring some of Augustine's decorations. "Wow, you're really good at this."

"She's an artist," I remind her. "When we have more time, I'll show you some of her work."

"My studio will be open for visitors tonight," says Augustine. "Just in case any potential customers show up."

"I think this is a multipurpose party," I tease as Liz and I leave.

"That's about the only reason my parents entertain," says Liz as we get into her car. "It's always about business and schmoozing."

"I'm not going to be like that when I'm grown-up," I say as I lean back into Liz's cushy leather seat.

Soon we're at the soccer field, yelling and screaming for our team, and I think our efforts are paying off, because by the end of the second half, it looks like they're going to win.

"Hudson is really good," says Liz after he scores a difficult goal. And, okay, something about the way she says this and the way she's looking at him right now seriously worries me. Now we haven't really said anything specific about this, but I assume that she knows *I'm the one interested in Hudson.* And it seems perfectly clear that Porter is extremely interested in her. He already ran up and hugged her when we got here. Oh, he hugged me too, but only afterward, sort of like a second thought.

Hopefully, we won't have any problems with this. Still, I'm not too sure, and it's undeniable that Hudson is hot. Especially in those soccer shorts. I mean, Porter is okay. He's cute and has a great personality. But Hudson is the only one I'm interested in. I reach into my hoody pocket and give my little white bag a hard squeeze, running the words of my ritual poem through my head five times. Numbers are important and meaningful. And I happen to know that the number five is good for challenges as well as passion. In fact, I've decided that it's my favorite number. And I don't think it's a coincidence that my birthday is the fifth day of the fifth month. That should make me very lucky in love. Still, I don't want to leave anything to chance. Certainly not Hudson Schwartz.

When the game is over (our team wins), the guys eventually wander away from their victory party on the field to join us.

"Thanks for coming and cheering us on," says Hudson.

"Hey, it was a lot more fun than cheering for the football team last night," I point out.

"Well, it must've helped," says Porter. "We weren't supposed to beat this team today."

"You guys are really good," observes Liz. "I'm impressed."

"And now don't forget your promise to come to my stepmom's party," I tell them. Then I hand Hudson a small card, where I've carefully written the address and the time. "Just so you don't get lost."

He laughs. "Hey, this isn't too far from where I live."

"Well, go figure." I act surprised, although I'm well aware of where he lives. I've known it for years.

Then we tell them good-bye and that we'll see them later, and we leave. I feel flushed with excitement as Liz drives away. I can't believe how well this is all going or how on track my life seems to be. Even so, I know that it's not just a coincidence or dumb luck. It's like I've taken control of things, and instead of my life running over me, I'm running it. And I think I'm doing a pretty good job too.

"See ya around seven," says Liz as she drops me off.

"Be ready to dance," I call as I get out.

"You too!"

Augustine doesn't seem as relaxed as when I left her. In fact, she's running around and acting pretty frenzied.

"Everything okay?" I ask.

"No!" she snaps. "The caterer was supposed to be here by four and I haven't heard a word from her and she's not answering her phone. Plus I'd planned on cleaning the bathrooms by now, but I got a call from my agent, and that took more than an hour, and now it's almost five and I haven't even had a shower and my hair is a — "

"Look," I tell her. "I'll clean the bathrooms. You go take a shower." I glance around the messy kitchen. "I'll straighten up in here too. And if the caterer calls, I'll find out what's up. Just relax and get yourself ready, okay?"

She nods and gives me a weak smile. "Yes, of course, I don't know why I'm getting all worked up about everything. I just want this to turn out perfectly. Do you know that we have about forty people coming?"

"That should be fun."

"I'll try to hurry."

"Take your time." Relieved to have her gone, I clean the kitchen first, just in case the caterer decides to show. After that I quickly straighten up the two relatively clean downstairs bathrooms. I'm guessing that upstairs will be mostly off-limits. But just in case, I decide to clean my bathroom too. I'm just on my way up when the caterer pops in through the back door, yelling, "Hello? Anyone home?" It's 5:45 and this woman seems a little harried too, but she's nice and apologetic. So I quickly show her around and help her unload some things from her van.

"Most everything is already prepared," she tells me as she slides a big aluminum tray into one of the preheated ovens. "I hope Augustine isn't too stressed by this. I did get her messages, but when I called back, the line was busy."

"She was on another call. Don't worry, I'm sure she'll be okay now that you're here," I assure her.

"Oh, thank goodness!" cries Augustine as she comes in to find the caterer fast at work. "I was so worried, I was making myself sick."

Then I excuse myself and leave the remainder of the party in Augustine's hands. I have no idea where my dad is right now, but I don't blame him for laying low. I think I'd have done the same if I'd known that Augustine was going to be so stressed by all this. After all, I remind myself, this party was her idea.

I treat myself to a bubble bath and a full beauty-treatment regime. Then I light some candles and take out my little white bag of what I'm now calling my "passion potion." I wish there was a way I could keep it with me tonight, but my outfit has no pockets and I don't need to carry a purse. The bag is too big to try to wear under my clothing. Then I remember a gold locket that belonged to Mom. She gave it to me before she died. I take it out and open it. Inside is a space that's big enough to hold a very small stone and some of the herb mixture. I carefully remove the picture of Mom that she put in it, tucking it into a corner of my jewelry box so that I can put it back later. I fill the inside of the locket with some of my passion potion and then fasten it around my neck. It actually looks nice against the black top. And I decide to wear some gold hoop earrings to go with it. Tonight I will wear my hair loose. I even take the time to curl the ends, which I think looks rather romantic.

As I go down the stairs I hear a low whistle, which I know belongs to my dad. I turn and make a mock bow, then thank him.

"You look lovely, Heather." He smiles and gives me a hug, then lowers his voice. "It's sweet of you to humor Augustine tonight."

I don't admit to him that I didn't do this for Augustine. "She's gone to a lot of work, Dad."

It's just getting dusky as Augustine and I light the little white candle jars that are hanging from the trees. "It's like a fairyland out here," I say as I look around. "Very pretty."

She nods with satisfaction. "It is, isn't it?"

"I like what you did with those leaves and branches," I say, pointing to one of her autumnal arrangements. "Clever."

"I thought we needed some color."

The jazz band is already warming up, and I have to admit that they're pretty good. Okay, maybe it's not a typical teen sort of party—not that I'd like something like that anyway. But I think this actually has a lot of class. I hope that Hudson doesn't think it's dumb. At the thought of him, I touch my locket and silently repeat my poem five times. Then I go down to the basement for a short break of centering exercises. I know that it's already past seven, but I feel the need to get in touch with my spiritual energy, a need to be empowered.

"Anyone down there?" calls a voice that sounds like Liz.

"I'm coming," I call back, turning on the light and blowing out the candles.

"What are you doing down here?" she asks as I meet her half-way up the stairs.

"Just meditating," I say.

"Cool."

"Yeah. It's a good way to relax and get centered."

"So are you?"

"Relaxed and centered?"

"Yeah. Did it work?"

I take in a deep breath and slowly let it out. "Actually, it did."

There are quite a few people here now, but Hudson and Porter haven't arrived yet. I hope they didn't change their minds. Liz and I hang together, and after a while, we actually get up and start to dance to a jazz song. We start out doing something that resembles the fox-trot, but it quickly turns into something more like jazz ballet. And when the song ends and we stop, we are surprised by the applause.

"More, more," calls out one of my dad's associates.

We both laugh, then gracefully bow, backing away from the dancing deck.

"That was really good," says another male voice off to our left. Then we turn to see Hudson and Porter standing in the shadows.

"Very well done," says Hudson. "Are you girls professional dancers?"

"We both do ballet," I tell them.

"We're ballerinas," says Liz with a cute giggle.

"It looked like you knew what you were doing," says Porter. "I know I'm impressed."

"So how about you guys?" I ask. "Do you know how to dance?"

"Not like that," says Hudson.

"Of course not," says Liz. "Now that would be weird."

"There's food and stuff in the kitchen," I tell them.

"And if you want to sneak some homemade wine," Liz says quietly, "I know where to get it."

I give her a look but don't stop them as they head over to the drinks table. I happen to know that my dad's pretty liberal about stuff like this. He has kind of a don't-ask-don't-tell policy. And I also know that he smoked marijuana in college. He just flat-out admitted it to me once. To be perfectly honest, it wouldn't surprise me if he and Augustine might sneak some grass occasionally even now. I'm pretty sure I smelled it on her once after she'd been down to the beach. But, like my dad, I don't ask and I don't tell either. In fact, if it wasn't for my friendship with Lucy and her very biblically based standards, who knows what I'd have done by now?

Consequently, I join my friends at the drinks table and, like them, I pour myself a little bit of Dad's boysenberry wine. To my surprise, it's much better than what he let me sample the other night. Then the four of us sneak off to a table in the corner of the yard and sit down.

"This party is really pretty cool," says Hudson.

"And the wine's not bad either," says Porter with a wink.

And so we just sit there, talking and joking, and I'm thinking this is all so surreal. Like, is this really my life? And before long, I'm not sure if it's the wine or Liz's persistence, but we're all four out on the dance floor, and these boys aren't half bad. Hudson is a fast learner and only steps on my toe once. My favorite songs are the slower ones, and I feel an amazing rush as he holds me close to him. I think I can feel the power of the locket between us. It's as if it's sealing something, and I'm pretty sure that Hudson can feel it too.

We switch partners a couple of times. I think it's just to be polite. And while Porter is actually a better dancer than Hudson, I can't wait to be back in Hudson's arms. Then, too soon, the party is winding down. The band plays a last song, and soon people start drifting away.

"I guess we should go too," says Hudson.

"This has been so fun," I tell him. "It's sad to see it end."

He looks directly into my eyes now. "I thought it was just beginning."

"Oh?"

He grins. "I mean, hopefully I'll get to see you again. How about if I call you tomorrow?"

"Sure," I tell him, trying not to sound overly eager. "That'd be good."

Then he leans down and kisses me good night, and it feels like my feet come off the ground.

"See ya later," calls Porter as the two guys make a quick exit out the back gate.

"That was fun," says Liz. "You guys need any help cleaning up?"

"No," says Augustine. "We're leaving everything for the morning. Then Vince gets to handle it. It's our little agreement."

I nod. "It's true. If one of them cooks, the other one cleans up."

"Augustine cooked all the food?" asks Liz, impressed.

"Not actually," I say quietly. "She had it catered."

"Smart woman."

"Hey, you could sleep over if you want," I say as Liz gets her purse. "I mean, I know you're home alone and everything."

"Thanks," she says. "That's tempting, but I think I'll just head home."

"Okay." Actually I'm relieved. I feel like I need some space right now. I want to think about everything that Hudson said and did tonight. I want to replay every little scene, maybe several times. And I want to do some rituals to ensure that whatever has begun will continue. And continue . . .

# nine

I FEEL LIKE I'M FLYING HIGH DURING THE NEXT WEEK. HUDSON IS STILL interested in me. We've talked and hung together and are going out tonight. Also, I've been doing better at ballet. I'm getting my strength back. I mean, it's like everything is going my way—and I know why. It's so amazing to have this new sense of control over my life, like I'm not going to be tossed around by uncontrollable circumstances ever again. It's incredibly freeing and exhilarating.

I'm beginning to understand why women from earlier centuries discovered and developed these kinds of powers. If you think about it from a historical perspective, women have been pretty downtrodden throughout the ages. It doesn't surprise me that this primarily feminine religion evolved and progressed. For instance, what if I'd been a Celtic maiden in the eighth century and my parents had promised my hand in marriage to the village brute? Well, I'm sure I'd have wanted to whip up a special potion to prevent that union from ever happening. Women had a need for magic or witchcraft or Wicca or whatever you wish to call it. I think it was a very necessary survival skill. I remember back when I used to argue with Lucy. I told her that Wicca was *not* a religion. But now I see that I was wrong. It's definitely a religion, and the deeper I get into it, the more I understand how powerful and exciting it really is. No wonder it's survived for so many thousands of years!

Thoughts about women in previous generations ripple through my head as I peruse the aisles at The Crystal Dragon. I've gathered a variety of items that I feel will be useful to my own practice. Among other things, I have a small gold-and-purple beaded pouch with a pentagram design that I plan to use for herbs and stones. But right now I feel strangely drawn to what looks like an Egyptian statue. I have no idea why, but I believe it has a spiritual connection to me, perhaps something from a previous life.

"That's Isis," says Willow.

"What?" I turn, surprised that the proprietress of the shop is here today. When I came in I saw only Jamie.

She smiles. "Sorry to startle you. I was speaking of the statue." She picks up the golden figurine and turns it slowly in her hands.

"Oh. Isis, is that her name?"

"Yes, Isis of a thousand names," she explains. "She's a goddess of magic and feminine power. It was through her that Osiris was restored to eternal life."

I nod as if I understand, but it's really Greek, make that Egyptian, to me. "She's very beautiful," I say.

"Those are hieroglyphics," says Willow, pointing to the base. "And that's onyx."

"Can you read hieroglyphics?" I ask.

She laughs. "No, but I suspect it tells the story of how Osiris' brother Set murdered him, sealed him in a special casket, and threw him into the Nile. Then about how Isis rescued Osiris and breathed life back into him. She had great powers."

"Wow."

"Of course, some dispute that story, telling the myth in a different way so poor Isis is left completely out of the story. I suspect that writer was a male, though." She strokes Isis's scepter. "Far too much history has been written by men."

"How much is Isis?"

Willow smiles. "Unfortunately, Isis is not cheap."

I nod and try to mentally calculate how much I've already gathered here today. I'm usually a rather frugal person. I got that from my mom. I know some girls who think nothing of spending more than $200 for a pair of shoes, including Liz, but I couldn't live with that kind of extravagance. Of course, this is different. This statue is worth more than shoes.

Willow sets the statue back on the glass shelf. "Isis is $185, Heather. I'm sure it's beyond your budget. But perhaps someday when you've—"

"No," I say quickly. "I want her. I'll buy her today."

Willow looks slightly surprised but simply smiles. "I'll have Jamie box her up for you."

"Thanks."

"But if you're getting Isis, it seems only right that you get a special altar cloth to set her upon. I would think something in purple, since Isis is such a powerful goddess. I just got some new ones in that are still in the box. Would you like a sneak preview?"

So I go to the back room, which I have been curious about, wondering if there is some wonderful magical setup back here. However, it's simply a very ordinary-looking back room.

"Here they are," says Willow as she sets a box on the table and opens it. "They come in purple and black. And the gilt moons and stars look amazing by candlelight. I saw one woman use it as a scarf too. Very pretty."

I'm not sure that I'd ever wear something like this as a scarf, and I can only imagine what someone like Lucy would say if I did. However, Halloween is coming. Who knows? "How much are these?" I ask.

"Only $20," she tells me as she unfolds a purple one, laying it in my hands. "Of course, they would be more if they were silk, but I do try to carry items that are affordable so everyone can enjoy the craft."

"Okay," I say. "I'll get this too. But I better stop here."

"Certainly."

As she writes up my purchases, she asks how I'm doing with my practice and whether I need any tips. "I'm having a special seminar two weekends from now. I think you'd benefit greatly from it, plus you would make some very good friends."

"Is it expensive?" I ask, suddenly concerned about the amount of money I'm spending.

"You have to think of these things as an investment," she tells me. "It's your life you're planning here, and you have to value it and know that it's worth putting time, energy, and yes, sometimes money into."

"So it's expensive."

She smiles. "I'll tell you what, Heather. Since you're new to the craft and I really do like you, I'd be willing to give you a discount again. If you decide you want to come, I'll take 20 percent off." She hands me a green paper with information on it. "The workshop includes one night's lodging, three meals, as well as the workshops and instruction—all for $300. But if you want to join us, it'll only be $240 for you. Oh, yes, and I almost forgot, everyone who comes to the seminar also gets a special discount coupon for 20 percent off any purchases made here within one visit."

I take the paper. "I'll think about it," I say.

"Well, don't think too long. Space is limited. I expect we'll be full in a few days."

I nod. "Okay. If I decide to come, can I just call to reserve my space?"

"Of course, dear."

Then I thank her and leave, but as I drive home I get a very strong urge to attend this seminar. I think Willow is right. It is my life we're talking about here. It's worth investing in. Still, I should probably discuss it with Dad, although I suspect he'll think it's silly or a waste of money. But I have a feeling Augustine will be okay with it. Maybe I should approach her first. She can talk Dad into anything.

Dad's car is gone when I get home, but it looks like Augustine is here. I go straight to her studio but then see she has company. This isn't unusual, since customers often come to her studio to talk about commissioned works or see what she has available. But she looks surprised to see me and sort of jumps when I call her name.

"Sorry to interrupt," I say quickly. "I wanted to ask you something, but I didn't know you had someone here. I can come back—"

"You're not an interruption." She puts a hand on my shoulder. "Heather, I'd like you to meet Jonathon Morrow, an old friend of mine. We went to school together in England."

He smiles and takes my hand. I notice how his dark eyes wrinkle at the corners, and it occurs to me that he's very good-looking, at least for a thirtysomething guy. "Nice to meet you, Heather." His accent is charming, and he sort of reminds me of Hugh Grant.

"You too," I say as he releases my hand. "Are you visiting in Westport or just passing through?"

"A bit of both," he says. "I'm quite charmed by your seaside town. I just happened into the Blue Moon Gallery and was stunned to see my old chum's art being shown there. Then I inquired about her and was even more stunned to learn that she actually lives in this quaint little town. The last time I saw her work was in a very chic gallery in Boston."

Augustine laughs. "Hey, so I finally figured things out. It's more fun to be a big fish in a small pond than a tiny fish lost in a big sea."

"Oh, I don't think that was ever the case." Then he turns and gives me a sad expression. "I was also a bit shocked to hear that Augustine recently married—I believe to your father. I didn't think this woman would ever settle down."

"Who says I'm settled now?" she teases.

I laugh. "Yes, *settled* is definitely not a word I would use to describe Augustine."

She nods. "Thank you."

"Nice to meet you," I say to Jonathon. "I'll talk to you later, Augustine. I'm going downstairs to practice for a while."

"I'll be here," she calls as I open the door to the basement.

And I really do intend to practice ballet down here, but I'm also very interested in practicing something else too. And I want to reexamine my new purchases. So I take them out. First I put the little beaded bag around my neck, and then I unfold and smooth the purple altar cloth, reverently laying it over my old toy chest. I'm amazed at how it immediately transforms the box into something rather magical. I light some candles and a stick of "energy" incense, then put on a new CD that Willow recommended. I open the cardboard box containing my precious Isis, carefully unwrapping the layers of tissue paper and finally setting her in the center of the altar cloth. I'm not sure if it's the music, the lighting, the mixture of scents, or Isis herself, but I am suddenly moved with a sense of awe.

I can feel the power in this room, and I invite the power to enter into my being. And after centering myself and recanting a chant that I created a few days ago, I remove my shoes and begin to dance. Not ballet, but more of a whirling, mystical, magical sort of dance—and it feels like an act of worship. When I finally stop, I am sweaty and out of breath. But I feel exhilarated, excited, and energized.

I don't think I could actually explain this euphoric feeling to anyone, not in a way that would make sense. I remember times when I was at Lucy's church and people were worshiping God. To be honest, I never really got it. I never felt like I was participating, just watching. But I do feel like I've been worshiping just now. Although I'm not sure who I've been worshiping. Not "God," since I've begun to question his existence. And I really don't think I'm worshiping Satan either. Maybe I'm just worshiping life in general.

"Heather?" I hear Augustine calling from the top of the stairs. "You down there?"

"Yes," I yell back. "I'll be up in a minute."

I turn on the lights and extinguish the candles and hurry up the stairs.

"It was so dark, I didn't think you were there," she says, looking at me curiously.

"Sometimes I like to dance by candlelight," I admit.

She smiles. "That sounds enchanting."

I nod eagerly. "It is."

She touches my cheek. "Your face is flushed, Heather. You must've danced up a storm."

I glance at the clock, surprised to see that it's close to six. "I didn't realize I danced so long, and I have a date with Hudson tonight. I probably should go clean up."

"Did you want to ask me something earlier?" she says as she

pours a glass of green tea, then hands it to me. "You should drink something."

"Thanks." So then I tell her about the seminar.

"Sounds interesting," she says, going over to look at the calendar on the refrigerator. "Hmmm, I think that's the same weekend your dad's going up to Portland to meet with that environmentalist legal beagle guy."

"Oh, do you think that'll be a problem?"

She turns and smiles. "I don't see why."

"Do you think Dad will mind if I go then? I mean, I guess I'm a little worried that he won't get it, you know? Sometimes he's kinda old-fashioned."

"Would you like me to talk to him?"

"Would you?"

"Of course. I think it sounds like a great opportunity for you, Heather. I like that you're taking an interest in new things." She pushes a strand of damp hair from my forehead. "You really seem to be coming into yourself lately. I think that's wonderful."

I finish my tea. "Thanks. It is pretty cool. I mean, I feel like I'm finding my real self, Augustine, sort of like you'd been telling me I would."

"I'm so happy for you, sweetie!"

"Thanks."

"Your dad and I are going to the little theater in North Bay tonight, a play about Oscar Wilde's mother."

"Sounds interesting."

"Hopefully."

"Well, have a good time," I call as I head for the stairs.

"You too."

After my shower, I'm trying to decide what to wear, and I'm

thinking I might try wearing the purple beaded bag as a necklace since it's really pretty. So I try it on with several things, but none of them seem to be working. Finally, I realize that it's close to seven and Hudson will be here soon, so I settle on a black turtleneck, which actually looks sophisticated and makes a nice backdrop for my purple bag. I fill this small bag with some of my special romantic herb mixture and then, remembering how well that little bit of potion in my locket has been working for me, shake it in as well. Then I go to my drawer for the tiny picture of Mom so that I can put it back in the locket, but I can't find it anywhere. I look and look, but it seems to be lost, and this troubles me.

"Heather," calls my dad's voice from downstairs. "Someone here for you."

I quickly put on some lip gloss, grab my jacket, and head downstairs. Pushing thoughts of the lost photo from my mind, I promise myself to search for it later. It couldn't have gone far. When I get downstairs, I'm slightly surprised to see that it's not only Hudson, but Porter and Liz as well. For some reason I thought it was just going to be Hudson and me tonight. But I smile at the three of them, acting as if this isn't unexpected.

"So what are we doing tonight?" I ask as I get into the backseat next to Hudson. It turns out that Porter is the driver tonight. "I know we talked about movies . . ."

Hudson chuckles. "Well, believe it or not, those two want to go bowling."

"Bowling?" I poke Liz in the shoulder. "Seriously?"

She turns around and grins. "Yep. Porter was telling me how he and Hudson used to go bowling every Saturday night when they were in middle school, and I thought it sounded kinda crazy and fun. I mean, do you realize that I've never been bowling in my entire life?"

"You've *never* been bowling?" I say.

"Nope. My parents think it's crass."

"Smart parents."

"Come on, Heather," urges Liz. "It'll be hilarious."

"Okay," I agree, "but I'll warn you, the last time I went bowling I was pretty pathetic."

"We'll help you," says Porter. "It's really not too complicated."

Hudson laughs. "Yeah, that's for sure."

So it is that we end up at Ebb Tide Alley, eating greasy pizza, wearing smelly shoes, and rolling heavy balls down a shiny floor.

"I wish I'd known what we were doing tonight," I say to Hudson after my slow-moving ball barely manages to knock down two pins, leaving five standing at the end of my turn. I push up my long sleeves and attempt to roll down my turtle neck, waving my hand in front of my face like a fan. "I would've worn a T-shirt."

He nods. "Yeah, you look a little hot."

I grin at him. "Gee, thanks. Just a *little* hot?"

He laughs as he picks up his ball. "No, you do look hot, but you look a little warm, too." Then he points to the beaded bag around my neck. "What's that thing anyway?"

I sort of shrug. "Just a necklace."

He gets ready to take his shot now, squaring himself up on the line and holding his ball out in front of him, just like he's told me to do about ten times.

"I think that bag has to do with magic," says Liz in a slightly teasing tone. "Did you guys know that Heather is learning about witchcraft?"

Hudson turns around and peers at me. "Seriously?"

I sort of laugh. "Hey, I'm just trying to tune myself into the universe. No biggie."

"Go on, Hudson," says Porter, "take your shot. Maybe Heather's magic will help you, 'cause right now, Liz and I are beating the socks off you two."

But Hudson's shot turns out to be a gutter ball. The first one he's had all night. "Looks like your magic isn't working for me," he says as he comes back to wait for his second ball.

I just smile at him. Maybe it's working better than he realizes. His second ball is only slightly better. It seems we're falling even further behind.

"Okay, Heather," says Hudson. "It's up to you now. Let's see if your magic really works or not."

So I decide to spiritually center myself as I stand on the line. I actually close my eyes and take a deep breath and focus. Then, imagining myself in perfect balance and the ball rolling straight down the center, I move forward and let it go. I stand there in amazement, watching as the ball does exactly as I'd envisioned, just like magic.

"A strike!" cries Liz, coming over to high-five me. "Maybe I should give your magic necklace a try too." Then she reaches for my bag and to my surprise gives it a little squeeze. Okay, I'm not an expert at this, but somehow I know that wasn't a good thing. Of course, I don't show that I'm irked by this, but when I take my second ball, after the pins are reset, I only manage to knock down one pin.

"Uh-oh," says Porter. "Looks like there's not enough magic to save you guys tonight."

And so he and Liz win our second line. Everyone except me thinks we need to play a third line. But I keep my thoughts to myself and try to be a good sport.

"Let's break up the winning team," Liz says to Porter. "This time I'll partner with Hudson, and you can be with Heather." And just like that we switch. Okay, I realize this isn't really a big deal, but it does bug me. Consequently, my bowling gets worse. And I must be rubbing off on Porter, because his does too. Meanwhile, Liz and Hudson are on fire.

"What's up with you guys?" asks Porter.

"I think Liz is good luck," says Hudson after his third strike.

"Guess I should've partnered with you," I say to her.

She laughs. "Who knew I'd end up being a bowler? But I love this!"

It seems to take forever, but finally we are done and I quickly take off my shoes, return them to the rental place, and head off to use the restroom. I take a moment to stand in the stall and center myself, repeating a relaxation chant in my head three times. Then I grasp the beaded bag and do the passion poem five times. Then I hurry out, wash my hands, and emerge from the restroom just in time to see Hudson giving Liz a hug. Okay, maybe it's a victory hug, but I can't help but think it's something more.

"Hey, you," says Liz. "We thought maybe you were a sore loser and had walked home without us."

"Yeah, right," I say as Hudson hands me my coat. "It'd be a long walk."

"Wasn't that fun?" says Liz as we go out to the car.

"I don't know," I say. "I don't think I'll ever be much of a bowler."

"We'll have to work on her, guys," says Liz, "cause I think I'm really into this bowling thing. I can even see me joining a league someday. I'll get my own ball, maybe in pale pink, and one of those cheesy shirts with my name on my chest pocket." She laughs. "My mom is going to freak."

"Ballerina turns bowler," says Hudson as Porter pulls out of the parking lot. "You might even make the local news."

The three of them laugh and joke about bowling and small towns and Saturday nights, and I know I'm being quiet, but it feels like something is wrong. Like something just broke and I'm not quite sure how to fix it. I just want to go home. Maybe I can fix it there.

I'm not surprised that Porter drops me off first. Hudson walks me to the door and asks if I'm okay. "You got kinda quiet just now."

"Yeah," I tell him with a forced smile. "I think all that bowling wore me out."

He laughs. Then I lean forward just slightly, expecting him to kiss me. It's how he says good-bye to me at school and after our last date. But tonight he surprises me by taking my hand. "Thanks, Heather. Tonight was fun." And that's it. Just like that, he turns and walks away. It's all I can do not to run after him. I want to apologize and say, "Sorry I was such a wet blanket tonight. I know I can learn to bowl better . . . and I can even learn to like it . . . and give me a chance . . . I'm just as much fun as Liz." But, naturally, I don't do this. I just walk into the house, go straight to my room, sit down on my bed, and ask myself, *What went wrong?*

And then it occurs to me, I need more power, a stronger magic. Obviously, I'm just a beginner in the craft. I need to be more disciplined. I need to learn more about the elements, the moon, the stars, the planets. I need more control.

# ten

"WANT TO GO WHALE WATCHING WITH US?" MY DAD ASKS ME THE NEXT morning. He and Augustine look like an Eddie Bauer ad in their matching blue nylon jackets and Chaco sandals. "I heard the big guys are heading down south right now."

"No thanks," I say as I pour a glass of orange juice. "You guys have fun though."

It's actually a relief to see my dad doing something just for the fun of it. Lately, he's been such a workaholic that I'm almost getting worried. After they leave and the house is extra quiet, I sit by the kitchen window, gazing out at the gray cloudy day. It looks just about how I feel, dismal and bleak. I know this is the wrong attitude. I can't give in to despair over the way things went last night. It's not the end of anything. I can't give up that easily. And yet I feel so hopeless. And lonely too. Sometimes I think Sunday is the loneliest day of the week.

There was a time when I went to church with Lucy on Sundays. Not every week, but sometimes. Enough so that people at her church seemed to think I was a Christian. But the truth is, I never felt like I really fit in. And last year I only went a handful of times. I can't even imagine going there now—or what Pastor Hamilton would think of me if he knew what I was into. I shove those unhappy thoughts away. I don't need that kind of negative energy right now. I should try to be around like-minded people, people who are willing to go outside the box and think for themselves.

I consider driving over to The Crystal Dragon and asking Willow for something special to help me through this challenge. But I have a feeling she'd tell me that I need to dig deeper within myself. And I suppose she'd be right. I probably just need to read some more, study some more, and record my thoughts in my Book of Shadows. I guess I just need more discipline. And so I commit myself to a day of discipline and ritual and learning. The power is within my reach. I just need to focus and learn how to access it and how to use it better.

I go down to the basement, but it feels as if something is wrong with the aura down here. Sure, it's okay for ballet, but I have a feeling that something about this room is not balanced quite right when it comes to magic. I think I need a place that's higher, loftier, closer to the sky and the constellations. So I carry all my tools and things up to my room, but then I don't think this is quite right either. Finally, I remember how much I enjoyed playing in the attic one particularly wet winter. Mom let me clear a place that was about ten feet square to use for my "special space," and it was quiet and serene and peaceful up there.

I decide to go up and see if Augustine has taken over the attic, and to my surprise my little clearing in the back is still there. Surrounded by the walls of boxes that Mom helped me stack is a wonderful secret place. Even the old pole lamp is still there, and it works. This secluded spot feels perfect. Well, other than some dust bunnies and spider webs, which I take care of. It takes three trips to haul everything up there, and it's not long until I have it all arranged and it looks really cool. Not only that, but it feels better. It

moon white | color me enchanted

feels right. I've placed an old Oriental carpet on the floor under my toy chest, which I covered with the altar cloth. On top of that is my statue of Isis and some candles and several of my favorite fairy figurines and other things. I light some candles and incense and move an old rocking chair near the pole lamp. Then I sit down and read for a while. Then I write for a while. And slowly yet surely, things start to make sense again.

There is a definite reason they call this religion a craft or a practice. I can see that it requires time and skill and learning and discipline. Today I focus on the Rule of Three. It's an ancient Wicca law that means whatever you do will be returned to you threefold. If you do good, you will receive three times as much good back. If you do evil, well, watch out! Of course, I'm trying to think of ways I can apply this principle to get Hudson back, since I'm fairly sure that I'm losing him. But other than making a new love potion, which I may or may not do, I have no ideas. And I have a feeling that the Rule of Three does not apply here. I think I need to put this guy out of my mind for the time being. I think the distraction is only stealing my good energy anyway. Still, it's hard. Truth: I'm not sure how to overcome it.

Finally, I think I've had enough study, and it's getting a little claustrophobic up here, so I decide to go to the WC for a Chai tea. I consider calling Liz, but I'm not entirely sure I want to see her. And when I check my cell phone on my way out to the car, I suppose I'm a little surprised that she hasn't called me.

Town seems pretty quiet today, typical for a Sunday when tourist season is pretty much slowing down. I order my Chai and go sit down at a table. I've brought along my Book of Shadows as well as one of my other books. I'm just starting to read when I hear someone say my name.

101

It's Sienna. She's wearing a brown coat that reaches nearly to her ankles, but she is smiling at me. "Want any company?" she asks as she blows the steam from her coffee.

"Sure," I tell her, although I'm not so sure that I want to be seen sitting here with her. Not that anyone is looking. Then I remind myself of the Rule of Three and figure I better be nice to her. Besides, those eyes of hers remind me of Mom again.

"That's a good book," she points out.

"Yeah, I like it."

"So you really are taking it seriously then?" She sips her coffee.

"Sure," I tell her. "Why wouldn't I?"

"Well, for most girls your age, it starts out as a fad. Or maybe something that gets a reaction from their friends."

"I don't really care what my friends think," I tell her. "Besides my ex-best friend, I've always been sort of a loner anyway. And she and I seem to be parting ways. She's kind of a religious freak."

"Some girls get into Wicca as a way to rebel against their parents." She peers at me now as if she's trying to see beneath my skin.

I sort of laugh at this. "You obviously don't know much about *my* family."

"Are you saying they're okay with this?"

I shrug. "Yeah. In fact, my stepmom is very supportive, and my dad's so wrapped in this big case that he doesn't have time to notice."

She nods. "So you're doing it for yourself then?"

"Pretty much so."

"Good for you." She takes another slow sip, then studies me. "Mind if I ask what kind of big case it is that your father is involved in?"

I shrug again. "Everyone in town knows about it," I say. "His firm represents the opposition to the development of Yaquina Lake."

Her brows lift as if she's impressed. "Your dad is Vince Sinclair?"

I smile. "That's him."

"Of Sinclair, Lewis, and Dey?"

"Yep."

"Well, my hat's off to them for helping to save the lake." She smiles. "I knew there was more than just one reason that I like you, Heather. I can sense these things. It's obvious you come from good people."

I'm not really sure how to respond, but I thank her.

"What about your stepmom, what does she do?"

So I tell her about Augustine's art, and once again Sienna is impressed. "I've met Augustine," she says with interest. "I went to one of her shows last summer. She's really good."

I nod. "Yeah, I know."

"And your mother died?" she says in a somber tone.

"Yes." I study her for a moment. "How did you know that?"

"I can feel the sadness around you, Heather."

"Really?" I divert my gaze from her eyes.

"Yes. From the moment I met you, I sensed an aura of sorrow." She sighs. "I'm sorry for your loss. How long has it been?"

So I tell her a little about my mom, how she was diagnosed with cancer when I was about nine and how she went through radiation and chemo and even some unconventional treatments but still died four years later.

"And when did your dad remarry?"

"Just a few months ago."

"And you're okay with Augustine? I mean, she seems like a good person to me."

"Yes. I like her."

"But you miss your mother?"

"Well of course." I look away again.

"And you've been trying to contact her?"

I look back at her.

She pushes a strand of graying brown hair away from her face and then smiles. I think I can see kindness in her lined face, a softness in her eyes. Then I nod. "Yeah."

"But you couldn't get through to her?"

"No."

"Do you want help?"

I consider this. I mean, a part of me desperately wants to reconnect with my mom, but another part of me doesn't want to be disrespectful of her or even of her death. There's no way I want to reduce the memory of my mom to a sideshow. "I'm not sure."

"I understand," says Sienna. "It's not the kind of thing I would push on anyone. I just got a very strong sense one day during your ballet class. I felt you'd been trying to contact someone and failing. I didn't know who, but the spiritual vibes were strong."

So I tell her about the time I went outside at night and did everything that I'd read to try to reach my mom. I explain how the writer compared making a connection to using your cell phone, and the steps I'd taken. "But it didn't work," I finally say. "Maybe she just didn't want to talk to me."

"Or maybe you needed operator assistance."

"Huh?"

Sienna smiles. "Sometimes your connection isn't going through because you need some outside help. You might need someone with more experience, someone with objectivity and the ability to pick up on things you might miss. Does that make sense?"

"Yeah, I think so."

"But I'm not pressuring you, Heather. I just like you and want to make myself available to you. It's hard being new in town, and I don't exactly make friends easily."

I remember the Rule of Three now and stick my hand out to Sienna. "Well, consider me your friend then, okay?"

She shakes my hand. "Thanks, Heather. I appreciate it."

Then I'm not sure what gets into me, but I open up and I pour out the story of last night and bowling and how my special potion seemed to backfire. And to my surprise, Sienna begins to laugh. I'm sure I look slightly stunned by her reaction, especially after I trusted her with something so personal.

"I'm sorry," she says, wiping her eyes with a napkin. "I'm not laughing at you, really, Heather. I just relate to your story. I remember doing something so similar to that once. Only I really made a total fool of myself."

"Oh." I guess that makes me feel just the slightest bit better.

She takes in a deep breath and seems to center herself. "And I've learned a lot since then. For instance, using any kind of love potion is usually unwise."

"Why?"

"Because you want someone to love you for who you are, Heather. It's not worth much if you charm them into it. Plus it can come back and bite you."

"Yeah, I sort of thought of that. I guess I just felt desperate. I so wanted him to like me."

"Well, I'm certainly no expert in the area of love and romance, but I suspect it's easier to attract someone when you don't appear to be trying too hard."

"I know, I know." I feel miserable. "I guess I just got caught up in the idea of having some power over things."

"Mostly you need to exercise the power over yourself, Heather."

"I know that too."

She nods. "Yes, we often know things in our heads, but our spirits are still learning."

"I guess."

"I'm sorry," says Sienna suddenly. "I didn't mean to lecture you."

"No, that's okay."

"Well, before I go, I should tell you about a gathering that might interest you."

"What's that?"

"Some of us are getting together at Yaquina Lake this evening at sunset. We want to perform a ritual to help preserve the lake, to save it from development."

"Who are *we*?"

"Just a handful of local people who understand the spiritual significance of this lake. Some environmentalists, some free spirits, and a handful of local Native Americans. It's a very diverse gathering, but you'd be most welcome. We plan to meet at the dock at around six. The ceremony won't be long, but hopefully it will help things. We're all very concerned about losing this lake."

I nod. "Yes. So am I. I'll try to make it."

"I've noticed that you've befriended the Daniels girl at ballet." She gets a curious expression now. "How's that going?"

I just shrug. "I'm not too sure."

"Well, be careful, Heather. Bad connections can drain your spiritual energy."

"What do you mean?" I study her dark eyes and wait.

"I mean, the wrong friends can bring the wrong energy. Sometimes you have to protect yourself." She unexpectedly puts her hand on mine for a brief moment, and I stop myself from pulling away. But this gesture seems almost motherly. Then she stands and leaves. I stay a bit longer, pondering some of the things she said. I have to admit this strange woman is growing on me.

When I get home there's a phone message from Dad and Augustine saying that they kept driving down the coast, "chasing whales" says Augustine. Consequently, they won't be back until late. I take this as a sign that I should go to Yaquina Lake tonight. Perhaps this is another chance for me to practice the Rule of Three by giving of myself. Hopefully these little steps will improve my karma. No doubt I can use all the help I can get.

There are about a dozen or so people at Yaquina Lake and I'm definitely the youngest of the bunch, but Sienna greets me and invites me to stand by her. To my surprise, it seems she's the one in charge. Her long, usually wild hair is twisted up in a bun, and she has a colorful scarf draped over the shoulders of her long brown coat. She actually looks fairly classy. As the sun sinks into the sky, we gather in a circle around a small fire. We burn candles and sage, and everyone takes turns blessing the lake, ending with some drumming music. One of the older Native American guys holds up his hands and speaks in what I'm guessing is his native tongue. And the whole thing is actually sort of cool and impressive, and I feel special to have been included. I just hope that this little event will help to preserve this lake. It really is a special place.

It's getting dusky as we walk back to the parking lot. Sienna walks with me, thanking me for coming.

"Thanks for inviting me," I tell her. "I'm really glad I got to come. I think my dad and stepmom would've liked it too, but they drove down the coast to whale watch today."

"Well, maybe we'll do this again," she says. "And hopefully with more people. But if we want our efforts to really have an effect, we must be careful to invite only those with a deep spirituality."

I nod and pull my car keys from my pocket. "Yes. I can understand that."

She pauses by my car. "Heather, I was thinking—after talking to you—and it occurred to me that you really need a guide or mentor. Perhaps you already have someone in mind, but I wanted to offer my services to you. I see such potential in you. Don't answer me now, though. Spend some time thinking about it. And please, know that I won't be offended if you choose another direction." Then she reaches over and pats me on the shoulder. "Take care."

I consider her offer as I go home. Maybe this is the path I'm supposed to take. I've certainly been frustrated and not exactly handling everything perfectly. Maybe Sienna really is my answer. Still, I won't decide until I'm home, back in my attic corner, where I can really weigh this and think.

# eleven

"Something happened," Liz tells me Monday morning. "I'm not quite sure how to explain it."

"What?" I ask, distracted by my locker, which is refusing to open.

"Well, Hudson came over to my house yesterday. I wasn't really sure why, but we just sort of hung and listened to music and talked and stuff."

I give my stubborn locker a hard hit with my fist, then turn and look at her.

"Don't get mad," she says, actually stepping back.

I force a smile. "I'm not mad." I nod to my locker. "It's just stuck."

"Oh." She sort of laughs. "So you're okay with it?"

"With what?" I ask as I attempt the combination again. This time I dial it very carefully, as if I'm counting to ten, and then it opens.

"About me and Hudson," she says.

I open my locker, retrieve my geometry book, then turn and look at her again. "What about you and Hudson?" I ask, looking straight into her eyes and thinking I want to make her squirm.

"Well, we sort of like each other." She glances away.

"Oh." I slam my locker shut.

"You're not mad, are you?" she asks, trailing behind me as I walk toward the math department.

I sort of shrug. "I guess I feel slightly betrayed," I admit, which is a huge understatement.

"I know," she says, "and I feel really bad. I mean, it's not like we planned this. But things happen, you know, sort of like chemistry. And if you like someone, well, you like them. It's not like we could help it, Heather."

I stop walking now and turn and look at her. "Fine," I say in a very stiff voice. "Whatever." Then I walk off. I hear her calling my name, but I just ignore her. Why shouldn't I? Friends don't do this to friends.

By noon, I'm still fuming. Oh, I try to act like I'm not, but I am boiling mad. I cannot believe Liz has stabbed me in the back like this. Or that she thinks I should just accept it as something that just "happened." And when I see her waiting for me in the usual spot at lunchtime, I am so furious that I simply turn around and go the other way. She calls my name, but I walk faster and eventually run. I duck through the library, then exit and go around the school and finally out to the parking lot, where I get into my car. Even though I don't have a pass, I drive away. I have no idea where I'm going or if I even care. But I just keep driving and eventually find myself on the coast highway, heading north.

It's a cold, foggy day, and I can't even see the ocean from the road. But maybe I don't really care. This isn't exactly a sightseeing trip. I think of my mom as I drive, remembering how she used to drive up the coast sometimes. "It helps me to think," she told me once, "sort of clears out my head." But it's not helping *me* to think, and as I hear my tires squealing around a corner, I realize that I'm not even paying attention to the road or my speed.

Feeling somewhat shocked at how irresponsible I'm being just now, I pull over to a viewpoint on the ocean side and stop, turn off the car, and get out. Then I walk around to the front of my car and actually begin pounding my fists into the hood. "Why is this happening?" I cry out over and over again. Then finally, after my hands are cold and beginning to ache, I quit and just turn around and sit on the hood of the car and blankly stare out to where the ocean should be, only it's shrouded in a heavy blanket of fog.

I wish I could talk to my mom right now. I wish I could ask her to tell me what to do, or what I'm doing wrong. I feel like such a loser. Maybe this whole Wicca thing is to blame. I don't know. It seemed to really work for me at first, like everything was under control and going so great. And now this. I don't get it.

Then I remember Sienna and her offer to help me. I remember how she even suggested I might contact my mom through her. Suddenly, it seems that she really is my answer. Why didn't I see it sooner? I pull out my phone and then realize I don't know her number. I can't even call information to get it because I don't know her last name. But I do know where she lives, and I decide to drive back to town. I realize she could be playing for a dance class, but then I also know that Naomi doesn't have that many classes this time of day since school's not out yet.

I park in the back, as usual, and go through the side door. I quietly go up the stairs, listening for music. But other than the sounds from the restaurant downstairs, the building is relatively quiet. I tiptoe past the second floor, worried that Naomi will pop out and question why I'm creeping around here when I should be in school, but I make it safely up to the third floor. I think Sienna said apartment three, but I'm not sure. I stop by the door and actually listen, and I think I can hear music in there. But I have to admit that I'm feeling spooked. It's pretty dim in this hallway, and the rundown appearance and old musty smell sort of gets to me. I quietly knock on the door, almost getting ready to run. But when it opens and I see Sienna standing there in front of what looks like a fairly normal, in fact a fairly attractive, apartment, I'm relieved.

"Well," she says, "I thought you'd come, but I didn't expect you this soon. Are you playing hooky?"

I kind of smile. "I guess."

"Come in." She opens the door wider and I go into what is a well-lit room with windows facing Main Street. Her style reminds me a bit of Augustine's, only I can tell that Sienna's is probably accomplished on a shoestring, whereas Augustine's funds sometimes seem unlimited.

"This is nice," I tell her.

She smiles and glances around the room. "I've fixed it up a lot. But I like it." She points to a couch covered in a colorful blanket that looks like it's from a Latin country. "Sit down."

So I do, and she sits across from me in a wooden rocker. "What can I do for you, Heather?"

So I just begin, once again, to dump on her. I tell her about Liz and how she's betrayed me, and how I drove up the highway a little recklessly, and how I wish I could talk to my mom, and how I feel pretty lost right now.

She nods. "I'm sorry you're having such a hard time. But sometimes it's the hard times that show us how to live our lives."

"Then you'd think I'd be an expert by now."

She sort of laughs. "It's what we do with our life lessons that changes us. And I have to admit that I'm not always the fastest to learn in my own life. I think sometimes it's easier to look at someone else and see where they need help."

"Well, I sure feel like I need help."

"What can I do for you?" She folds her hands in her lap and waits.

"I was thinking about your offer to sort of teach me," I begin.

She nods and waits.

"I think I'd like that."

"Good."

"And . . . also, I was thinking about my mom . . . and how you said maybe you could contact her . . ."

"I can't promise anything, Heather. But I can try."

"Uh, do you charge anything . . . I mean to contact the dead? I read that some people do . . . that it's kind of a business."

She frowns. "I don't agree with that. I think if you truly have a gift, you should use it to help others, not to make money."

I nod. This is reassuring.

"There are a couple of ways to do it," she begins. "Sometimes it works with just a couple of people, and sometimes it helps to have a small group. It also helps to have an item that belonged to the person we're trying to reach, or to be someplace where that person enjoyed being." She looks at me and smiles. "Of course, since you're here, that could be enough in itself. I'm sure your mother would want to communicate with you."

I reach for the locket that I'm wearing today. "This was hers," I say as I unlatch it. "I did have a photo of her in it, but I seem to have lost it." I shove down a wave of guilt for losing my mom's photo, but I've searched everywhere and it seems to have totally disappeared.

"Yes, that will be helpful."

I look around the room and wonder what my mother would think of this. Then I remember something. "My mom always loved being in the dance studio," I say suddenly. "She loved watching me dance."

Sienna nods. "Well, then maybe we have enough to work with right here. Do you want to give it a try?"

I feel sort of nervous now. "I guess so. I mean, if you think it's okay. I don't want to push things. This is all so new to me."

"Don't worry. It's really not such a big deal." She's walking across the room toward the bank of windows now. "It does help me to concentrate if I pull the drapes, though. Do you mind?"

"No."

So she pulls some dark blue, thick velvet drapes shut, and the room instantly gets very dim. She goes over to a round table covered in a paisley cloth and lights some candles. "We'll work over here," she says. "And I'll put on some music. Sometimes it helps me to relax better, and to tune out the distracting sounds from the street." She pushes a button, and some flute music mixed with the sound of chimes begins to float through the apartment.

I sit down at the table, and she brings a black velvet bag over and reverently opens it and removes a shiny black bowl.

"What's that?" I ask in a quiet voice.

"It's a scrying mirror," she tells me, carefully setting it in the center of the table. "Sometimes I can see things in it."

I look at the black surface and wonder why it's called a mirror.

Sienna takes a deep breath, then slowly exhales. She does this several times and then sits down across from me and places both of her hands, palms down, on the table. Then she leans over and looks into the bowl.

I sit and wait for a long time, and finally Sienna speaks. "Did your mother have a flower name, sort of like yours?"

"Yes," I say quickly. "It was Lillian, but she went by Lily."

"Uh-huh."

I'm impressed, but then I realize that Sienna might've learned that from someone in town, maybe even Naomi, since she and my mom were pretty good friends. Yet somehow I don't think so. Sienna strikes me as someone sincere. And, I remind myself, she's not doing this for money.

"I want you to focus on your mom," she says.

"Okay."

"Set the locket on the table," she tells me. "It might help to get her attention."

So I set the gold heart next to the bowl, carefully arranging the chain so that it looks nice.

"Good." She takes another deep breath and exhales. "Now think about your mother, Heather. You can try to picture her face . . . or just think about a time that's special to you, something you two did together . . . something happy."

"Okay." And so I imagine Mom and me walking on the beach, looking for shells and agates or interesting pieces of driftwood.

"Good." She takes in another breath, holds it, then slowly lets it out. "I think I'm seeing something . . . your mother was a pretty woman."

"Yes."

"Not dark-haired like you, though?"

"No."

"Fair-haired."

"Yes."

"Petite."

"Yes."

"A quiet spirit."

"Yes."

"Dark eyes?"

I nod without answering, but my hands are shaking.

Now there's a long silence, and I guess it worries me. I wonder if something's wrong. Is my mom sad? What does it feel like to be dead?

"Your mother loves you very much, Heather."

I nod. Of course. I know this. At least I think I do.

"But she's worried about you."

I nod again, swallowing against the lump in my throat.

"She doesn't want you to be lonely, Heather."

"Yes?"

"And she's worried that you're going to be hurt."

"I *have* been hurt," I remind her. "Just today."

"Yes, but I think it's something more than that . . . it seems like she's talking about something that hasn't happened yet . . . something that's troubling her."

"Okay." Now I'm thinking this is not such great news. I mean, I've already had a cruddy day. Are things going to get worse? "Do you know what she means exactly?" I ask.

"I'm not sure." She peers into the black bowl and just looks. "I feel it has to do with a close relationship."

"Like Liz?" I ask. "Or Hudson?"

"No." Another long pause. "I think it's someone in your family."

"Family?" I consider this, thinking I'm a little short on relatives. "Who do you mean?"

"I'm not sure."

"Oh."

"I'm getting something else . . . oh, yes, I see."

"What?"

"Your mother doesn't want you to give up dance."

"Oh."

"Were you considering that?"

"Well, sort of." Okay, I was really considering it today. I know that I'm not looking forward to spending *any* time with Liz anytime soon, and it'll be hard to avoid her at ballet.

"Your mother wants to see you dance the Sugar Plum Fairy."

"To *see* me?" Okay, that's encouraging because I'd love for her to see me dance that part. But I also want to point out that may not happen, whether or not I give up dance, but it seems sort of irrelevant right now. I mean, I'm just glad that Mom *wants* to see me or *can* see me — that it's even possible. That's reassuring somehow.

"Something else, Heather."

"Yes?"

"She wants you to know that she's okay."

"Really?" I feel tears coming now.

"Yes. She thinks you've been worried about her, and she wants you to know she's happy."

"She's *really* happy?" My voice breaks and hot tears slide down my cheeks.

"Yes. She says you don't need to worry about her. She's where she needs to be and she's very, very happy there. She wants you to be happy too."

"Oh." Now I'm not sure how to react to this. I mean, I'm glad Mom is *very, very happy*. But I'm thinking I'm not there with her, and yet she's still happy. I can't quite wrap my head around that. Doesn't she miss me? Sometimes I miss her so much that it physically hurts inside.

Sienna takes in another long breath and slowly lets it out. I hear the sound of chimes and almost jump, but then I remember it's just part of the music she's playing. "I think that's all," she says softly. "For now anyway."

I just sit there, trying to absorb everything I just heard. My mother is worried about me. She thinks I'm going to be hurt by a family member. She wants me to keep doing ballet, and she's very happy to be where she is.

"But where *is* she?" I ask as Sienna opens the drapes again.

"Where is she?" she echoes.

"Yes. You said she's very, very happy and she's where she needs to be, but *where is that?*"

"The other side, of course."

Of course.

Sienna looks at her watch. "I have to play for a lesson in about twenty minutes and I need to do a couple of things first."

"Yes," I say, standing. "Sorry. I should go."

She pats my shoulder and hands me a tissue. "You don't need to be sorry, Heather."

"Okay." I use the tissue to wipe my wet cheeks.

"And I'm glad you came by today. But you really should go back to school now. I'm sure your mother would agree."

I attempt a smile. "Yes, I'm sure."

"And anytime you need to talk, please, feel free to pop in. I play for lessons from two in the afternoon and as late as nine on Mondays and Wednesdays. The rest of the days I'm usually done by seven and, as you know, Saturdays are only until five and Naomi doesn't have classes on Sundays."

"Yes," I reply. "I'm sure I'll come to visit sometimes. Thanks again."

"By the way, you're going to doubt this later," she says as she walks me to the door. "That I really contacted your mother today."

"Really?"

"Yes. Everyone does. So I'll tell you something else. It didn't seem terribly significant, not in light of her concern and the warning about getting hurt. Consequently, I'm not sure that I got it exactly right. But maybe I should tell you anyway."

"What is it?" I say eagerly, grateful for any small morsel of information.

"She said that *her book's not lost*—or something to that effect."

"Huh?"

"I don't know how to explain, but that's pretty much what I heard."

"Her book's not lost?"

"That's right."

"I don't get it."

"Well, it might be metaphorical."

I consider this. "Maybe." Then I thank her again and leave, going as quietly down the stairs as I came up. But just as I reach the second floor, I run straight into Naomi.

"Heather? What were you doing up there?" she asks with obvious curiosity.

"I . . . uh . . . I was at Sienna's." I cannot believe I just blurted out the truth. But what else could I say?

Naomi frowns. "Why?"

"We were just visiting."

"What about school?"

I shrug and look away.

Naomi puts a firm hand on my shoulder. "Heather, be careful of Sienna. I really don't know much about her—or her beliefs."

I blink in surprise. "What?"

She locks eyes with me. "Just be careful. Understand?"

I nod, then tell her I have to go. Feeling confused, I get in my car and drive back to school. Why is Naomi suddenly interfering with me — first my diet and now my friends? What business is it of hers anyway? And, for someone who tries to keep her opinions to herself, I'm surprised she'd say something like that about her own employee. Pretty judgmental if you ask me. I decide to dismiss her warning altogether. She just doesn't get it.

Once I'm at school, still remembering my mom and wondering if she's watching me right now, I go straight to the office and explain to Mrs. Aster, the office lady, that I had "a problem" and had to leave at lunchtime, suggesting it was of a feminine nature and had to be dealt with.

"I understand," she says as she writes out an excuse. "Sometimes it's hard being a girl." Then she winks at me.

Okay, I'm sure if I did this sort of thing on a regular basis, I wouldn't get this kind of sympathy. But my attendance record has always been pretty good. And my grades are well above average, so I guess they figure they can cut me some slack. Fine with me.

I still feel bummed about what Liz did to me, and I try to keep a low profile until the end of the day, when I get out of there as soon as the last bell rings. I don't look right or left and don't even go to my locker. I just go straight to the parking lot and into my car. I am not the least bit eager to see Liz or Hudson anytime soon. I'm sure they feel the same way about me.

# twelve

SOMEHOW I MAKE IT THROUGH TUESDAY WITHOUT RUNNING INTO LIZ OR Hudson. But I am stopped by Porter.

"So what do you think of the news?" he asks me.

"Huh?" I decide to play dumb.

"You know," he says in a slightly irritated tone. "Liz and Hudson hooking up. Whad'ya think of it?"

I just shrug. "Whatever."

He scowls. "Really, you're okay with it then?"

I study him for a moment, realizing that, like me, he's probably been hurt. And then I remember the Rule of Three and I think, hey, maybe it's worth a try to be nice to someone. Although to be honest, I don't think the Rule of Three's been working too well for me lately. "I guess there's not much anyone can do about it," I tell him. "Are you feeling pretty bummed?"

He sort of rolls his eyes. "I'm not really talking to Hudson yet."

"So you were really into Liz then?"

He gives me this *duh* look. And I wonder why I even asked. Of course he was into Liz. She's pretty and fun and even a good bowler. Why wouldn't he be into her?

"Okay, I guess that's a yes."

"So are you and Liz still talking?"

I shake my head. "It's just kinda awkward," I admit.

"Yeah, that's how I feel." Then he brightens a little. "Hey, maybe you and I should get together."

"Thanks," I tell him. "But I'm not really ready for anything right now." Okay, I'm mostly not ready for anything with him. Besides that, I'm not even over Hudson yet. I caught a glimpse of him on my way to Creative Writing today, and it was all I could do not to start crying again.

Porter kind of laughs. "I thought maybe if we got together it might make them jealous."

"Yeah, right." I let out a loud sigh.

"Well, believe it or not, I thought Hudson was really into you, Heather. He talked about you a lot. The weird thing is that he's a pretty conservative guy, you know, but he thought it was cool that you're so different."

"Different?"

"You know, into witchcraft and ballet and your artsy family and stuff. He was pretty cool with that."

"Apparently he wasn't totally cool with it." I frown. "Or maybe it was just me."

"I think maybe he got overwhelmed," says Porter.

I stand up straighter now. "Well, maybe it's for the best," I say. "But it would've been nice if he and Liz had handled things differently. They didn't have to go behind our backs like that."

He nods. "Yep. That's what I think too."

"I gotta get to geometry," I tell him.

"See ya."

As I walk away, I wonder about what he just said. Is it possible that I really did overwhelm Hudson? Was he really as into me as Porter was saying? Oh, it's not like I want to get up false hopes, but suddenly it occurs to me that this thing with Liz could blow over if he finds out there's not that much to the girl. Or not. But I suppose it does give me just a smidgen of hope to know that Hudson really was into me. Maybe this isn't over yet.

After school, I go straight home again. Day number two without talking to Liz or Hudson. Of course, there's still ballet to come. I'll have to face her there. As I drive home I try not to think about the feelings that ran through my mind earlier today. I saw Liz eating lunch with my old friends, including Lucy, and I wanted to scream. I mean, it's like she's replaced me or something. It was weird. And for a moment, I felt as if I really hated her. I felt like she was ruining my life. I told myself that was stupid. But then, later on, when I saw her with Hudson, laughing and holding hands, well, I wanted to throw up.

And now as I park in my driveway, I think this girl must really be set upon ruining my life. First of all she tries to take my spot in ballet. Next thing I find out that it's her dad who wants to ruin Yaquina Lake, the lake Mom and I enjoyed so many times. Not to mention that it's my dad who's turned into a workaholic trying to oppose this senseless development. Then Liz pretends to befriend me but goes behind my back and steals my boyfriend. And finally, it seems that she's taking over my friends. Seriously, what more could anyone do? The next thing I know she'll probably sneak into my house and kill me in my sleep. It's just too weird.

I think about what Sienna said yesterday, about how my mom was worried that someone was going to hurt me. Well, if you ask me, Liz has done a pretty knock-up job of it so far. Still, Sienna seemed fairly certain that it wasn't about Liz. But how can that be? I've never had a real enemy before, not that I can recall anyway, but I'm beginning to feel like I have a serious one now. Oh, sure, Liz may act all sweet and kind on the exterior, but I have a feeling that beneath that pretty blonde veneer of sugar and niceness, there's a heart of stone—an ice-cold heart of stone.

I know enough about witchcraft to know that it's wrong to try to invoke harm on anyone. I've read that again and again. And yet I've also read some websites where they dispute this, saying that the first rule is to harm none, but that you are allowed to use magic against your enemies. And I think that maybe it's time to get serious. I dump my bag and head straight for the attic, getting a book where I've seen the recipe for what's called a "witch's bottle," a tool that's supposed to protect you from your enemies. I search in the book until I find it, and it actually seems rather simple—even if it is a little bit gross. But desperate times call for desperate measures, right?

So I go down to the kitchen and hunt down a small jar and lid. Then I go out to the garage to look for sharp and dangerous things to fill it with. You need things like nails, tacks, razor blades, needles, pins—anything that could hurt someone. It takes a while, but finally I have it about half-full of some nasty-looking things. Okay, now for the gross part. To make this work, you have to urinate into the jar. Enough said.

After this is done, you're supposed to tape it up and bury it at least a foot underground in a meaningful and significant place. And I know just the place. I drive over to Liz's house, up on the bluff. But I park down below, at the end of the beach access road, and I go out to the beach, then walk down a ways until I find a secluded spot where the bluff meets the sand. It's straight down from Liz's house. Perfect. I forgot to bring a shovel, but I use a stick and my hands, and before long I dig a hole that's almost two feet deep. Then I stand up and repeat some lines that I've written down, words that are meant specifically for Liz, my enemy. And I bury the jar and brush off my hands and leave.

Of course, all this makes me a few minutes late for ballet. And naturally, this means that I'm just a little bit off in everything. And, once again, Liz dances beautifully and I feel as if I'm trying to keep up. It's particularly aggravating when she goes out of her way to smile at me, which feels fairly patronizing and makes me want to hit her. Also, I can feel Sienna watching me as she plays the piano, and I'm guessing she feels bad for me too. In some ways, I suppose I should appreciate the sympathy, since I think hers is sincere. But just the same, I avoid making eye contact with her. Besides, I have this sneaking suspicion that she might not approve of my witch's bottle. I'm not sure that I'll even tell her about it. Maybe it will be my little secret. There could be more power in that.

As soon as class is over, I grab up my stuff and dart out of there. I don't want to talk to anyone today. Mostly I don't want to talk to Liz. I go straight home and I'm heading into the house when I see Augustine's friend Jonathon Morrow coming out. He looks like he's in a hurry, but he waves at me as he hops into a small blue and very cool BMW convertible.

"You're home early," says Augustine as I come into the kitchen. She's putting what looks like two wine glasses into the dishwasher.

"I didn't know Jonathon was still in town," I say.

"Oh yeah," she says in an even voice. Her back's still to me. "He really likes Westport. He's actually thinking about staying."

"Cool," I say, although I'm wondering if it's really that cool. I mean, what does this mean? Jonathon hanging around my dad's wife, the two of them drinking wine in the middle of the day when no one's home. If you ask me, it's a little fishy.

"Hey, I talked to your dad," says Augustine. She turns around and smiles. "And at first he wasn't too excited about it."

"What?" I say, unsure of what she's referring to.

"You know," she says, "about the Wicca seminar that you asked me about."

"Oh yeah," I say. "I almost forgot."

"Well, he had a lot of questions, but I think I got them smoothed over. I told him it's all part of your spiritual exploration and that we need to allow you to grow into your spiritual self with as much support as possible. He seemed to get it."

"So he's okay?"

She nods.

"Thanks," I tell her.

"And," she says dramatically, "we're going to pay for it too."

"No way," I say.

"Yep. I told him that I was going to pay for half of it, and he didn't want to be outdone. He'll pay for the other half."

"Cool," I say, although I'm actually having second thoughts right now. What if I don't want to go? But I keep this to myself.

"I still have that brochure," she says. "It's in my purse. I actually called the woman, I think her name's Willow or something. And I reserved your spot. She said I was lucky, because they only had two spots left."

"Thanks," I tell her.

Augustine laughs. "Willow even tried to talk me into coming."

"Why don't you?" I ask, thinking I wouldn't mind having someone I know there.

She waves her hand. "No, I don't want to infringe on this for you, Heather. It's your experience. You need to do it on your own."

"Well, thanks," I tell her again. Then I get myself a bottle of juice and head upstairs to think about this. I suppose it's a good thing she did this, but for some reason that I can't even put my finger on, it bugs me that she went so far in making all the arrangements. Maybe it's just that I wish I'd done it myself. But then I remember what a shambles my life's been the past few days. No wonder I forgot. I guess I really should be thankful that Augustine was on top of it, especially since I don't really feel like I can get on top of anything at the moment.

Somehow I make it through the remainder of the week. I feel like I'm in survival mode, and I'm sure I must walk around school looking like a total grump. More and more, I don't really care what people think of me. I'm sure everyone spends too much time worrying about what others think of them. The truth is, everyone is probably just thinking about themselves anyway.

By Saturday, I feel like I'm drained. Just trying to navigate the emotional minefield of my life is exhausting. But the more I think about it, the more certain I am that Liz is at the root of all my problems. She's tried to speak to me several times, and finally I just had to tell her to knock it off.

"You are not my friend," I said in a surprisingly calm voice on Thursday afternoon. "I have no reason to talk to you. Please leave me alone."

She just sort of blinked and then turned and walked away. But after that, I couldn't help but notice something. I'd catch her from the corner of my eye talking to someone—someone like Hudson or Chelsea or Kendall. I even spied her talking to Lucy on Friday at lunch and they both nodded. Liz was holding her hand over her mouth as if she thought that was discreet, then she glanced at me and quietly said something to Lucy, but I know she was talking about me. I think Liz has set out to totally ruin me.

On Saturday morning I drive up to North Bay. I probably would've gone to see Sienna, but I know she's working. Once again

I'm on a mission. But Willow is not there today. There's only silly Jamie, and she's pretty useless. Even so, I feel desperate and I decide to give Jamie a try. I mean, what can it hurt? Maybe she knows of something in the back room.

"Uh, Jamie," I say in a quiet voice. There are a couple of other shoppers here. "Do you know of anything that I can use against an enemy?"

Her eyebrows shoot up. "Huh?" she says, looking at me suspiciously.

"Never mind," I say, quickly turning away and walking over to the candle shelf. Why did I even bother?

I'm about ready to give up when I feel this nudge on my elbow. I turn to see a young woman with jet-black hair, the kind of black that you know has been dyed. Her eyes are outlined in black too—thick, sharp lines that make her look a little scary. She's wearing a beat-up black leather jacket, which only adds to the drama. I'm guessing she's older than me, probably in her twenties. I'm about to ask her if she wants something when I notice a black tattoo of a pentagram on her right hand. And suddenly I feel tongue-tied.

"Are you looking for something?" she says quietly.

"What?" I ask, unsure of what she means.

"I heard you asking the clerk about something for an enemy."

"Oh." I just shrug. "I was just joking."

She peers into my eyes now. "I don't think you were joking. But if you were, well, I won't bug you." Then she simply walks out of the store.

Now I feel like maybe I've missed a real opportunity. Maybe this girl really knows her stuff. Maybe she can help me. I quickly exit the store and look down the street, seeing her standing in front of a shop window.

"Excuse me," I say as I go and stand next to her, looking in the window at the porcelain figurines of lighthouses. "I didn't mean to sound rude, but I don't know you and I'm really a beginner in all this, and I probably shouldn't be trying to do a spell against an enemy yet."

She turns and looks at me with those outlined eyes, just looks for several seconds, then says, "That's right."

Okay, now I don't know what to say and I feel stupid. "Sorry to bother you," I say, leaving.

"Wait," she says, and I stop. "Want to get some coffee?"

So I agree and we go into a little coffee shop on the corner. We get our drinks and then sit down in a quiet corner. She gives me only her first name, which is Jane. So, feeling a little cautious, I only give my first name as well. I'm just not sure where she's coming from—not sure if I should even trust her.

"Heather is a good name," she says, blowing the steam off her espresso. And suddenly she lightens up and begins to talk just like an ordinary person. "I don't know why I spoke to you like that in Willow's shop," she says. "I mean, it's really none of my business. My boyfriend, Eric, says I'm always butting into things that I should stay out of. I suppose it's because I'm slightly psychic. I feel for others, empathy, you know."

"It's okay," I tell her. "I probably felt sort of embarrassed for even asking about something like that in the first place. I mean, I know about the rule of harming none."

"But you do know the next line don't you?"

"What do you mean?"

"I mean in the Wiccan Rede."

"What's that?

"Well, you know the Threefold Law, right?"

129

"Of course. You mean the Rule of Three. I know it has several names, but it's always the same meaning."

*"Mind the Threefold Law, you should, three times bad and three times good."*

I nod. "Yes, I know about that."

"And you know the rest of it too?" she asks. *"Eight words the Wiccan Rede fulfill: An it harm none, do what ye will. Blessed be to thee."*

"Yes, I've read that before too, but I haven't memorized it yet."

"Well, some interpret 'do what ye will' as 'do what needs to be done.' Sometimes we need to use our power to set things right. Sometimes you must take control of a situation before it gets out of hand, before someone, even you, gets hurt."

"Yes," I say with some enthusiasm. "I do feel like that in my situation."

"That's what I thought, Heather."

So I open up, and like letting the cork out, the whole story comes tumbling out. I tell her all about Liz and all the things she's done to upset my life.

"Wow, that is some bad karma."

I nod and take a sip of Chai tea.

"And her dad is that guy who wants to destroy Yaquina Lake?"

"The same."

"And your dad is trying to preserve it?"

"Yep."

"Talk about the forces of good and evil colliding, Heather. No wonder you feel so beat up."

"That's exactly how I feel." I just shake my head. "I really hoped that Willow would be in her shop today. I have another friend back in Westport, but she's working today. I just wanted some help. It's like I've been in this horrible battle all week and I'm so tired of it."

"But you've been practicing all week, right? You haven't slacked off, have you?"

"Not at all. Last night I was up until one in the morning."

"Good. Some novices just want to give up when things get tough. But that's what separates the real ones from the fakes. And I sense that you're real."

I nod. "I'm serious about this. I mean, I've seen and experienced things that are totally amazing. I believe in it and I've experienced the power. I even signed up for Willow's seminar next weekend. I wish it was this weekend instead."

"Lucky you." Jane lets out a frustrated sigh. "I wish I could go too, but there's no way I could afford it. Besides, I work that weekend."

"Oh."

"Hey, don't feel bad for me. I've had lots more experience than you. And I've had some good teachers. I probably don't really need to go. I just thought it would be cool."

"Right."

She leans forward now, looking intently into my eyes. "I want to help you, Heather. And your situation reminds me of something that really worked for me a couple of years ago." Then she tells me about an abusive stepfather and how she put a curse on him. "A woman who's been practicing for years gave it to me. A few weeks after I used it, my stepdad was fired from his job, got a horrible case of shingles, and it wasn't long before he left my mom. She's so much better off without him."

"So it really worked?"

She nods solemnly.

"Wow."

"I still have the recipe, but I swore never to give it to anyone."

"Oh." So I wonder why she is telling me about this. Just to rub it in?

"I could probably make it for you, but only if I'm absolutely positive that you're really serious about everything you've just said. I mean, this isn't something to toy around with, you know. It's powerful."

"I *am* serious," I tell her, although to be perfectly honest, I'm not so sure this is a good idea.

She studies me for a long moment. I get the feeling she's trying to discern whether or not I'm trustworthy. And for some reason this makes me want to convince her. But I just sit there, saying nothing.

"I suppose I could put it together for you. And I'll need to buy some things." One of her brows arches. "The thing is, I'm pretty broke right now."

"How much do you need?"

"Thirty should do it."

Okay, now I'm having some doubts as I get into my purse. I mean, how stupid is it to give a virtual stranger $30 to do something like this? Even so, I hand her a ten and a twenty.

She pockets the cash, then looks at the clock over the counter. "Can you meet me at Fletcher's Cove at . . . say, two?"

"Sure," I tell her, wondering if she'll actually show up.

"Okay, see ya later." And then she leaves, and I'm pretty sure I won't be seeing her or my thirty bucks again. But I suppose it's a relatively cheap lesson for a beginner like me. What a sucker! I don't think I'll be telling either Sienna or Willow about my little lapse of sense. I go out and look down the street for Jane, thinking maybe I could tell her I've changed my mind. But she's nowhere to be seen. Big surprise there.

So I walk around awhile, then finally get into my car and start driving toward home. But then I wonder, what if Jane is legit? What if she's really concocting some special potion right this minute, really going to some trouble for me? And what if she makes the trip to Fletcher's Cove and then I'm not even there? That doesn't seem very nice on my part. Especially if she was really trusting me. I know how it feels to be betrayed. I don't really want to put someone else through that. So after driving halfway home, even though I know it could be a waste of time and gas, I turn around and drive back toward North Bay. I exit at Fletcher's Cove and park by some trash cans. Then I just sit in my car and wait. It's only a few minutes, but it seems like hours before it's finally two and then, just as I originally feared, no one shows up. I guess I really am a sucker.

I wait until exactly 2:07 and then, feeling like a complete idiot, I decide to give up and leave. But just as I turn the key in the ignition, I see an old red pickup come in on the other end of the pullout. Then Jane, still wearing her black leather coat, hops out of the passenger side and runs over to my window. Her dark hair is whipping in the wind, and she's carrying something close to her chest.

"Sorry I'm late," she says slightly breathlessly. "But Eric didn't get off work until one, and I needed him to drive me here." She hands me a small burlap bag along with an index card. "Whatever you do, do *not* open this bag, okay?"

"Okay."

"Now this is what you do," and then she explains how I need to get a small item that's been in contact with Liz. "It could be a piece of clothing, a snip of her hair, a pencil, whatever. Then you put this bag along with the item in another bag and you say the words on the card, then burn the card. After that you hide the bag somewhere where you know this girl will be, even if it's only for a short time. But she must be within a yard of it."

"Like where do I put it? And then what if she sees the bag and opens it? Or what if she figures it out?"

"I know, it's tricky. You definitely don't want her to open the bag. Can you slip it under her mattress? Or put it in her car?"

I frown. "I don't know."

"Well, I put it in my stepdad's car, and it worked like a dream."

"I'll see what I can do," I say.

"And then you have to retrieve the bag and then bury it within a mile of where she lives."

"Man, this is complicated."

She frowns. "Did you expect something this big to be easy?"

"Well, no."

"You don't have to do it, Heather. You could just sit back and do nothing. Just passively wait until this girl manages to destroy your entire life."

"No," I say quickly. "I don't want to do that."

"It's up to you."

I nod. "I know you're right. And I'll figure out a way to do it. Thanks for doing this for me. I really do appreciate it."

She smiles now and I see that she's actually pretty in a witchy sort of way. "No problem," she says. "We have to help each other, you know. We need to stick together."

Then she runs back and gets into the pickup, waving from the open window, and they drive away. I set the burlap bag on the passenger seat and hope that it won't hurt me before I have a chance to hide it somewhere. But even as I think this, I question whether I can really do this. I mean, doesn't this break the Rule of Three? But then I consider what Jane said about stopping someone before they do more harm. I think that's the case with Liz. She must be stopped. And perhaps this will even work to stop her dad. I can only hope.

# thirteen

I FEEL A SENSE OF EXCITEMENT AND HOPE AS I DRIVE BACK TO WESTPORT. AND I've barely driven a mile before a plan begins to present itself to me, starting with a way to get a personal item from Liz. I remember how she likes to leave some spare dance things in a locker at the dance studio. "Just in case I forget to bring my bag to school," she told me once. "Then I don't have to drive all the way home to get it." So I drive to town, park behind the studio, then go up the stairs and over to the short row of lockers that are set up near the bathrooms.

I can hear Sienna playing piano and Naomi calling out positions as I try to remember which locker Liz uses. I asked her once why she didn't bring a padlock for it, and she just laughed. "Who'd want my sweaty leotard and these old toe shoes?" I guess I know who. I just hope they're still here. To my relief, I find her bag in the second locker I check. I quietly unzip the bag to see her faded pink toe shoes right on top. One of the ribbons looks like it's already pretty loose, so I give it a hard jerk and it pops right off. Then I put everything back as it was before and, pocketing the ribbon, head back to my car.

Then I go home and prepare to finish the spell. I'm not sure what to use for the other bag. I'm thinking something inconspicuous, just in case I don't retrieve it in time and she finds it. I finally settle on a brown lunch sack. Hopefully it'll just look like trash. Then I put it together and go through the steps that Jane told me and, after repeating the words and burning the card, I call Liz and tell her I need to talk. "I know I've been acting pretty juvenile," I tell her. "I guess it might help if we talked about it."

"Yes," she says eagerly. "I agree totally. I'm so glad you called. It's really been bugging me."

So I suggest that she meet me at the jetty. My plan is that I'll have to get into her car so that we can talk out of the wind. Once I'm in her car, I'll somehow slip the bag underneath the seat. I don't know how I'll retrieve it later, but I guess I don't need to worry about that yet.

"Why the jetty?" she asks.

"Well, I need to drive over to North Bay for Augustine," I lie. "The jetty's on the way for me, plus it's not far from your house. Is that a problem?"

"No."

"I'll be there in about ten minutes," I say.

"Okay."

I start feeling nervous after we hang up. Maybe this is crazy. Maybe I shouldn't be messing with something I don't totally understand. But I keep telling myself what Jane said about how it's okay to stop someone from harming you. Isn't that just what I'm doing?

I don't see Liz's car in the jetty parking lot, but this gives me time to get my wits together. Also, I slip the brown bag inside my coat, on the right side, hoping that somehow I'll be able to discreetly slip it under the seat. I get out of my car now, leaning against the door on the driver's side for some protection against the wind that's whipping through here.

By the time Liz gets here, I really am cold from standing in the wind. I wait for her to get out of her car, then walk over and meet her halfway. We both just stand there for a couple of seconds and then, just like magic, she asks if I want to sit inside her car to talk.

I nod. "Yeah, it's pretty cold out here. I think it's about to rain."

I go straight to the passenger side and am actually inside before she is. As she's opening her door, I slip the bag beneath my seat. I can hear my heart pounding, afraid that she might've noticed, that she might ask what I was doing, and what would I say? But she just sits down, then turns in her seat to look at me.

"I'm really sorry, Heather," she says before I can say anything.

I sort of shrug. "Well, I just thought you should know that what you did really hurt me. A lot."

"I know that Hudson and I should've handled it differently," she says. "But everything happened so fast. And I just wasn't thinking."

"I'll say."

"But, like Hudson told me this week, you guys had only gone out a couple of times. It's not like it was really serious."

"It was still wrong," I tell her. "I thought you were my friend, Liz."

"I am your friend."

I stare at her for a moment, thinking about how she's been my object of hatred this past week. "How can you even say that?" I ask.

"Because I want us to still be friends," she says. "I mean, we have ballet, and I'm friends with your friends. You need to get over this—"

"*I* need to get over this?" I say loudly. "You go behind my back, you steal my boyfriend, and you tell me that *I* need to get over this?"

She doesn't say anything now, just looks down at her lap.

137

"Seriously, Liz. What did I do to deserve this?"

"I didn't do it to hurt you, Heather. It just happened. What do you want me to do now? Should I break up with Hudson?"

I consider this, saying nothing.

"It's not like it would change anything. He said he didn't want to get back together with you anyway."

"He said that?" I study her for a moment. I think she's lying.

"Something to that effect."

"Well, that's not what Porter told me."

She sighs and just shakes her head. "Can't you see that you need to move on, Heather?"

This girl has a lot of nerve telling *me* to move on. She's the one who moved in on my space, moved to my town, moved in on my boyfriend and my friends. She's moved into my spot in ballet, and her parents even want to move in on a lake that I don't want to see destroyed. How dare she tell me to move on?

"The only thing I need to move on from is you!" I snap as I reach for the door handle. Then I swing open the door and leap out of her car, run over to mine, and ignoring her pleas to come back, I get in and drive away so fast that my tires spit gravel behind me.

My heart is really pounding as I continue to speed down the highway. I feel as if I just committed a crime, although I know that's ridiculous. So I tell myself to calm down, to just breathe, and I attempt to center myself. I go directly home and straight up to the attic, where I then perform some cleansing rituals and a few other techniques that I hope will keep me on track. I have to admit that what I just did is unsettling. And because I respect and appreciate the power I have, I really don't want to abuse it. I hope I haven't. But the truth is, I feel very uneasy. Worse than that, I feel afraid.

By Tuesday of next week, nothing out of the ordinary has

happened. Liz has not been struck by lightning (which is actually a relief), but neither has she, as far as I can see, experienced an ounce of discomfort. And in ballet, she dances more beautifully than ever, like a pro. Whereas I'm so distracted over all this silly hocus pocus that I forget some easy steps and fumble about and pretty much wish I hadn't even come today. I purposely came late, hoping that by some chance Liz's car would be unlocked and I could sneak the bag out and go bury it later. But no such luck. I wonder if it's still there. What if she found it? And what if she knows that I'm the one responsible?

I can sense Sienna looking at me when class ends, almost as if she'd like to talk to me privately. Does she suspect that I've done something? Should I tell her? Or would that simply complicate everything? Perhaps the spell will be more effective if kept secret. I wish I knew Jane's phone number so I could call and ask. As it is, I don't even know her last name.

By Thursday, my stomach is seriously bothering me. I almost wonder if I could be getting an ulcer. Even more frustrating is that I still can't see that Liz's life has been impacted by all the effort I put into that stupid potion. Maybe the thing doesn't work until after it's buried. If anything, Liz seems happier than ever. She and Hudson are still together. She's still hanging with my old friends. And, like insult to injury, she and Lucy actually appear to be hitting it off, which I think is so weird. I mean, those girls are total opposites—how can they even stand each other? I start to wonder if maybe they're doing it just to get to me. And then I realize how paranoid that sounds. Even so, I skip ballet. My excuse is my stomachache, although I don't admit to Augustine or Dad that I didn't go. I don't really think it's their business. The only reason I don't quit altogether is because of what Sienna told me—that my mom doesn't want me to quit.

And I believe that's true.

By Friday, I'm starting to think that maybe I'm going crazy. I mean literally, flipping-out, lock-this-girl-up crazy. This paranoia thing seems very real. It's like the whole world is plotting against me. I think I see kids talking about me, pointing at me, laughing at me. It seems like my teachers are picking on me. It's like nothing is as it should be. Then, as I'm driving home from school, I remember the Rule of Three and I'm afraid that the evil I tried to invoke onto Liz is being turned on me—times three. And I am freaked.

But I try to block out all this negativity as I pack my things for this weekend's seminar. And I tell myself that this is going to be a turning point for me. Things are going to change. I'm going to discover how to really use the power, the magic—but only in good ways. I've learned my lesson. And after this weekend, my life is going to improve drastically. To be honest, it doesn't seem like it could get much worse anyway. I gently shoo Oliver from my room. The last thing I need is for him to get trapped in there while I'm gone. One time he broke several of my fairy figurines trying to escape out the window.

"You all ready to go?" asks Augustine when I come downstairs with my stuff.

"Yeah."

"I wrote down the number of the place," she says. "I got it off the brochure. Just in case your cell phone doesn't work and I need to reach you. The location sounds a little isolated."

"But interesting," I point out. "I've always wanted to see the inside of that lighthouse as well as the keeper's house. It looks so mysterious from the road."

"I heard that it's haunted," she says with a sly smile. "Sounds like fun."

I nod. "Yeah, I hope so."

"You're not having second thoughts, are you, sweetie?"

"No," I say quickly. "Of course not. I think I'm just tired."

"Well, maybe this weekend will refresh you."

"Yeah, maybe."

"Your dad called just a few minutes ago. He was just getting into Portland, said the traffic is horrible."

"Guess he should be glad he doesn't live there."

She nods. "He said he missed you this morning and to tell you to have a good time this weekend and to bring him home some eye of newt."

"Yeah, right." I glance at the clock. "Well, I guess I'll head out. They have registration, then dinner."

Augustine gives me a big hug. "Have fun, okay? Make it a really good weekend."

I force a smile. "I will. And thanks for getting Dad on board with it and everything." Then I tell her good-bye and head out to my car. But as I drive up the coast, I really am having second thoughts. I mean, what makes me think I can do this? And what if everyone else is really accomplished and I'm like "Heather, the Teenaged Witch"? I actually used to like that Sabrina show, back when I was like thirteen. Now I just think it's dumb. Still, I don't want people thinking I'm dumb too.

I do some centering exercises as I drive. About halfway there, I pull over to write some things down in my Book of Shadows. Some things that I think are fairly profound and encouraging. And by the time I turn at the lighthouse, I'm feeling just slightly empowered, and I'm thinking maybe I can do this after all.

"Hello, Heather," says Willow when I go into the main building. "Welcome."

"This is such a cool place to have this," I tell her as I set my bag on a chair.

"It's very special." Then she hands me a paper. "This is the list of the classes and workshops. You're early enough that you can pretty much take your pick."

"Sienna McKay?" I say as I glance over the paper.

"Yes," says Willow. "I haven't actually met her, but she was recommended to me by an associate. He told me that her powers as a clairvoyant are impressive."

"Is she from Westport?" I ask hopefully.

"Yes, I believe that's right."

"I think I know her," I say. "She plays piano for my dance teacher."

"Good. Maybe you'll want to sign up for her séance class tomorrow. It's considered advanced, but I think you can handle it."

So I do sign up for that as well as some that sound more basic. Then I hand it back to Willow. "Does that look okay?" I ask.

"Very good," she says as she glances over the paper. "Here's your room number and key. You'll be rooming with a young woman from Vancouver. Her name is Caroline, but she hasn't arrived yet. And there are refreshments in the parlor. Dinner is at seven."

I thank her, then set off to find my room. It turns out to be on the third floor, which I'm guessing was once the attic. It reminds me of my secret space at home. I pick the twin bed closest to the dormer window and put my things into the old oak dresser next to it. Hopefully Caroline won't mind. I catch a glimpse of myself in the slightly cloudy mirror and realize that I look pretty much like a high schooler. Okay, that's what I am, but I don't need to advertise this fact. So I remove my T-shirt and replace it with my black turtleneck sweater, then I pull my hair back and put it in a twisted bun. I slip in some silver hoop earrings and stand up straight, and I think I should be able to at least pass for being in college.

Then I sit in the straight-backed chair by the window and look out. The view from up here is amazing. And although it was overcast earlier today, the clouds all seem to have blown away now, and I can see the ocean stretching out in layers of blues that eventually blend into the sky. I decide to use this quiet time to write in my Book of Shadows, describing the feeling of this house, this room, the view, and pondering over the spirits who may still be dwelling here. I get some goose bumps on my arms as I consider the possibilities, but it's not like I'm really scared. More just intrigued.

"Hello," says a female voice with a tap on the door. "I'm Caroline, your roommate."

"Come in," I call out, closing my book and looking up.

A short and slightly stout redheaded woman comes in and dumps several bags onto the floor with a loud thud. "Good grief, someone should've warned me there were three flights of stairs to my room."

"With an exceptional view," I point out.

She glances over this way, then flops down on her bed and exhales loudly. "I'm dying for a cigarette," she says, suddenly sitting back up. "Do you mind if I smoke?"

Actually I do mind, but I hate making a fuss. So I just shake my head and watch as she fumbles through her purse until she locates a pack and her lighter.

"I'll try to keep the smoke over here," she says.

"Maybe I can open the window," I suggest. But after a couple of tries, it's obvious that it's been painted shut.

"It took nearly four hours to get here," she says, fanning her smoke away from me with a magazine. Like it's really going to make a difference in this small room anyway.

"Willow said you're from Vancouver," I say. "I assume she meant Washington State and not BC."

"Definitely Washington. BC would be a really long drive. Just the same, I'm beat." She's using a paper coffee cup as an ashtray, and I'm starting to worry she might burn this whole place down. I wonder if smoking is even allowed, although I don't recall seeing any signs. Still, you'd think she might set off a smoke alarm.

"Well, dinner's not until seven," I say, standing. "Maybe you can have a rest. I think I'll go down and see what they have to snack on."

"I think I will catch a little catnap," she says, blowing out a long puff of smoke.

I want to warn her to be careful and not to burn down our room, not to mention this entire historical house. But instead I just slip out and go downstairs. There I meet several women and, to my surprise, a man named Dylan who lives up the coast. For some reason I didn't expect there would be any men attending. But I suppose that's rather prejudicial on my part. It's obvious that I'm the youngest one here, but I don't actually confess my age. I'm afraid they won't take me seriously if I do. Even Willow doesn't know that I'm only sixteen. Perhaps age is gauged differently in this particular circle. Maybe I'll be accepted simply because I'm one of them. And when I'm offered a glass of wine at dinner, I don't refuse. Maybe it will make me appear older.

# fourteen

I'M TRYING TO KEEP AN OPEN MIND, BUT THE TRUTH IS, A PART OF ME THINKS A lot of this is just a little bit weird. I mean, simply because a person wants to tap into the energies and power of the universe, does that mean she needs to act like a freak? Okay, to be fair, not everyone here is acting freaky, but some are. And, although I try to hide it, their behavior aggravates me. This is the kind of stuff that gives us a bad name. For instance, there's Sylvia from Salem. This middle-aged woman seems to delight in shocking people. Her language is very coarse and graphic, and although I hear stuff like that at school a lot, it's particularly skanky when you hear it coming from someone my dad's age. Sylvia has informed everyone here that she's been a witch for nearly thirty years. "Back when witchcraft wasn't in vogue," she's pointed out several times. Like it's in vogue now? But I can tell she's very proud of her history. And, really, that's fine. What bugs me is that this woman stinks.

It figures that I'm the one who gets to sit next to her at dinner. She's wearing this long black crushed-velvet gown with tangled fringe around the sleeves and hem, and it honestly smells as if she's worn this garment for years without ever having it cleaned. Seriously. It reeks of foul-smelling body odor. It doesn't help that I have a fairly sensitive sense of smell. A week or so ago, Willow told me that's a good thing, that it will help me to identify and understand the elements of various herbs and their powers. She said it's important to tune all your senses into the world—that's what makes you good at your craft. But at the moment, all I can smell is Sylvia's body odor. I wonder how she's managed to utilize all her senses for so many years while smelling worse than the guys' locker room.

After dinner, which is sadly unappealing due to the aroma next to me, Willow gives us a welcome speech and then we do some "get acquainted" exercises, which are actually kind of interesting.

"This place has great vibes for a weekend like this," Caroline says to me during a break. I went outside for some fresh air, and she came out for a quick cigarette. Now, I don't want to be rude and walk away from her, so instead of inhaling the clean sea air, I'm breathing secondhand smoke.

"I can't wait to hear the speaker tonight," I say.

"Yes, I've read about Marie Van Horn. She's a renowned expert on channeling," says Caroline. "I'm into it myself. I have a definite gift, but I'm still something of a novice. It'll be so exciting to hear from someone who has a real handle on it."

"Do you think she'll actually attempt to channel someone tonight?" I ask, shivering in the cool sea breeze.

"I hope so. They say this place is haunted, so I'd think someone like Marie would have no problem. I know I've been getting plenty of vibes already."

"Really?"

"Oh yes. Just walking up the stairs this afternoon, I definitely felt the spirit of a young woman. I think she was crying."

"Oh."

"Guess we should go in now. It's almost time for the speaker." Caroline snuffs out her cigarette and we go back in through the

French doors. The group is just gathering in the meeting/dining room. I make sure to find a seat that's well away from stinky Sylvia. Although someone has lit some scented candles and incense, and that seems to help. I'm not sure if they did this for the atmosphere or to help eradicate the smell, but it's working for me. Caroline and I take seats on the left side of the room, waiting for the speaker to make her appearance.

Then the lights are turned down, a woman steps up to the front of the room, and everyone gets quiet, expectant, waiting. This woman stands at the wood podium, near the flickering candles, just waiting for a long moment, gazing across the small group as if she's taking us all in, perhaps evaluating us. I wonder what she sees, how far beneath the surface. I sit up straighter.

Marie Van Horn is a dramatic-looking woman. Not so much in a weird way, like Sylvia, but in an artsy way. She has on black pants and a sweater accented with a colorful silk scarf and stone jewelry, and her gray hair is neatly pulled into a French twist. She wears tortoise-shell half-glasses, and her voice is slightly theatrical as she tells us a bit about herself, how she first discovered her divining gifts at an early age, and how she's spent most of her life honing them and trying to use them to help others. She's written several books, which are for sale this weekend, and she has a popular website. All in all, impressive.

"As you know, I'm from the East Coast. I've never been in this part of the country before. But already I've experienced a number of spirits in this house as well as in the lighthouse." She says this in a quiet tone, which makes everyone seem to lean forward and listen more intently. "One spirit in particular seems to be speaking to me—a young woman whom I believe has been trapped here against her will. Even now she's crying out for understanding."

Caroline gently nudges me with her elbow, giving me a little nod, which I'm guessing is to acknowledge that this is the same spirit she experienced earlier today.

Marie closes her eyes now and tilts her head back. There is a long pause, and the room is so quiet I'm sure you could literally hear a pin drop. And a shiver goes straight down my spine and I'm actually sitting on the edge of my seat, almost afraid to breathe.

"My name is Annabel," says Marie in a voice that's higher pitched and younger sounding. "Please, help me. Help me . . ." Marie takes in a slow deep breath and waits. "I came here with my friends one night . . . long, long ago. Henry said the lighthouse was haunted . . . we only came to explore . . . we were playing a hiding game . . . and I went into a closet and I became—I was—" And now Marie is sobbing. Actually sobbing. But not like a woman of her appearance. She reminds me more of someone my age, someone who's falling apart and nearly hysterical. I almost can't look at her because this seems too private, too personal, like we shouldn't be gawking at something like this. But, like everyone here, I keep watching.

*"Someone pushed me!"* says Marie suddenly and we all jump. "Two hands placed firmly on my shoulders, pushed me from behind . . . and I went forward and then down, down, down . . . and then it was black and quiet and no one was here . . . no one but me. They left me alone and I cannot get out of this house. I need help. Please . . . where are my friends? Why am I here? Why is it so cold?"

Suddenly a breeze passes through the room and one of the candles goes out. Everyone seems to take in a sharp breath at the same moment. And then the lights are turned back on, and Marie returns to her normal self. Another woman I haven't met, but I'm guessing may be Marie's assistant, rushes to her side, puts an arm around her, and helps her to the closest door.

"Thank you, Marie," says Willow as she hurries to the podium. "It takes a lot of energy out of Marie to channel a spirit like that. What you've just seen is a real treat. Not every group gets to experience something of that magnitude. Hopefully Marie will be able to communicate with Annabel some more before she leaves tomorrow. I know that I, for one, want to hear the rest of this story."

Now the woman who helped Marie returns to the room and steps up to the podium and Willow introduces her as Fiona, Marie's partner.

"I will be selling Marie's books in the parlor tonight and in the morning," she tells the group. "Marie will be available to sign them for you tomorrow. But for tonight, you must excuse her. This was a very emotional connection, very draining. Marie must rest and regain her energy. But she asked me to tell you that you were a very responsive audience. She believes that's why Annabel felt comfortable enough to reveal herself to us. Thank you!"

Then we clap and Fiona leaves. Willow makes a few announcements and then we're dismissed.

"I've got to get some of those books," says Caroline. "That was so amazing."

I nod. "I think I'll wait until tomorrow," I say. "Right now I'm just plain tired. I think I'll go to bed."

"I'll try to be quiet when I come in," says Caroline.

I really am tired, but more than that I'm ready for a break. Being around all these strange people and trying to soak all this in, well, I think I can understand why Marie feels so drained. Oh, sure, I wasn't channeling, but I did feel extremely involved. And I'm sure that I could feel Annabel's spirit too. Still, it's a little overwhelming. I feel like I need some time to myself.

I get ready for bed, but before I do, I decide to write in my Book of Shadows. I turn on the light next to my bed and begin to write. And the strangest thing happens as I write. It's as if someone else is writing for me. At first I think it's Annabel, but then I'm not so sure. It seems more like a guy's voice. But I allow it to continue, barely noticing the words that are flowing from my pen, and finally I'm done and I feel totally exhausted, like I cannot keep my eyes open. So I set the book on the bedside table, turn off the light, and go to sleep.

I wake up to the sound of someone desperately crying. It's dark in the room, and for a moment I can't remember where I am. I fumble for the light and finally manage to get it on. Then I see that it's Caroline. She's in the bed next to me and she seems to be having some horrible dream. I don't know whether to wake her up or just let her keep crying. Perhaps she's channeling.

"Caroline?" I say quietly as I stand over her bed, unsure of what to do.

Still, she thrashes and cries out words that I can't quite make out.

I reach down and touch her shoulder. "Caroline?" I say again. "Are you okay?"

And now she sits up and opens her eyes, but it really doesn't look like her. I mean, she still has red hair and everything, but her eyes look wild and sort of vacant and she screams obscenities at me and looks as if she'd like to kill me and I am so scared that I'm shaking. I've never been this scared in my life. She keeps on screaming and I go for the door, ready to run for my life!

In the hall, I nearly collide with another guest. "What's going on in there?" asks a quiet young woman I met earlier tonight, I can't remember her name. She's in a pale blue flannel nightgown and looks nearly as frightened as I feel.

"It's my roommate, Caroline," I say breathlessly, nodding back to my room. "She's kinda freaking. I don't know what to do." Then this woman's roommate, an older woman named Averil, comes out blinking in the hallway light, and we explain what's going on.

"She's probably talking to a spirit," says Averil. "That can happen in your sleep, you know."

"What do I do?" I ask.

She considers this. We can still hear Caroline yelling in there. It's a good thing there are only two rooms up here, or she might awaken the whole house.

"I don't know if we should wake her," says Averil.

"Is that dangerous?" I ask.

"I'm not sure."

"Maybe we should talk to her," says Averil. "See if we can sort of ease her out of it."

"I'm not sure that I want to talk to her," I admit. "She's pretty scary."

Averil sort of laughs. "I'm not afraid."

So as we follow Averil back to my room, I whisper to the other woman that I can't remember her name.

"Rebecca," she tells me. "I'm not as brave as Averil."

"You and me both," I say.

We stand in the doorway, watching as Averil tries to reason with Caroline, or whatever it is that seems to be inhabiting Caroline. And, honestly, it feels like a scene right out of *The Exorcist*. I know because Augustine and I watched it on the old movie channel just a couple of weeks ago.

Finally, Averil shakes Caroline, who wakes up and immediately begins to sob. Then all three of us go in and sit around Caroline's bed, asking if she's okay and if we can get her anything.

"It was so horrible," she says as she wipes her nose with a tissue. "I can't explain it, but it was horrible."

"Were you channeling?" I ask.

She just shakes her head. "I don't know . . . I'm not sure. This happens sometimes, usually when I'm very tired or have been through something emotional. But I don't know if it's channeling or not."

"Do you remember what you said?"

"No." She looks down at her hands. "I'm sorry if I said anything bad. I know that happens sometimes. My mother told me I said some horrible things in my sleep once, when I was home for Christmas."

"Are you able to go back to sleep now?" asks Averil.

Caroline nods. "Yes, I'm so sorry for bothering everyone."

"It's okay," says Rebecca. "I hope you can sleep now."

"We have a couple of hours before it's time to get up," I point out.

So we all say good night, and I get back into bed, turn out the light, and attempt to go to sleep. But I can't. I'm wide awake now. And I can feel that whatever was troubling Caroline is still lurking somewhere nearby. Definitely in this house, and possibly even in this room. I really want to get up and turn on the light, but it sounds as if Caroline has finally gone back to sleep and I don't want to disturb her. So I just sit up in bed and wait for morning. It feels like the longest two hours of my life, and by the time I see the gray dawn in the window, I'm exhausted.

Still, I get up and get dressed. Feeling like a zombie, I go down to breakfast. Caroline seems perfectly fine, almost as if nothing happened last night. And even when I see Averil and Rebecca, they act totally normal. I almost start to think that I imagined the whole thing. I feel dull and lethargic as I go to my first morning workshop.

It's on herbs and minerals, and I keep myself awake by taking lots of notes. After that, I go to Sienna's class on séances. But, again, I have a hard time focusing. Willow is in this class too, as an observer, she points out at the beginning. And midway through Sienna's class, Willow challenges her on something to do with her technique. I'm not totally sure what it was because I probably wasn't paying as close of attention as I should.

"I think it's different with everyone," says Sienna. "You have to find what works best for you."

"But you're here as the expert," points out Willow. "Surely you can be more specific than that."

Sienna looks a little miffed. "As the expert," she says in an irate voice, "I'm saying that speaking to the dead is very much an art, and like any other form of art, it can be subjective. Is that clear enough for you?"

Willow narrows her eyes now. "I suppose if that's the best you can offer us. I suppose I'd expected a bit more."

Sienna looks hurt now. And I feel sorry for her.

"Sienna made contact with my mother," I say quickly. Everyone in the workshop turns and looks at me now. "It was really amazing," I continue. "And to be honest, I was a little skeptical at first. But I could tell it was the real thing. And when we got done, I was pretty amazed."

Willow gives me a questioning look, then stands, excuses herself, and leaves.

After the workshop, Sienna takes me aside, speaking quietly. "I hate to say this to you, Heather, but Willow may not be all that you think she is."

"What do you mean?"

"I mean I don't trust her."

"Oh." Of course. Why should she when Willow obviously took an instant dislike to her? But I don't say this.

"Anyway, I just wanted to warn you to be on your guard against her—"

"Against who?" says a woman's voice from behind us.

We both turn to see Willow in the doorway.

Sienna stands up straight, looking Willow in the eyes. "Against you," she says to Willow.

"How dare you?" says Willow, taking a step closer to her.

"I've heard things about you," says Sienna now. "I tried to put them out of my head because it seemed like you were helping Heather, and then you invited me here. But now that I've met you . . ." She glances at me. "I know what I've heard is true. And since Heather's my friend, I want to protect her."

Willow laughs. "You want to protect Heather? You should think about protecting yourself. I've heard about you too."

"What?" demands Sienna hotly. "What have you heard?"

Willow shrugs. "Nothing that needs repeating."

"That's because you've heard nothing."

"That's because I know how to keep my mouth shut," snaps Willow. "Hopefully you will do the same."

Sienna just glares at her now.

"I assume this is good-bye then," says Willow. Then she adds sarcastically, "Thank you so much for teaching your workshop. Your check will be in the mail."

Sienna gives me a glance, then storms out.

"Watch out for that one," says Willow. "She's trouble."

I don't know what to do now, so I do nothing. Then Willow leaves and I look out the window in time to see Sienna loading some things into her old van. I decide to go out and ask her what's going on.

"That just happens sometimes," says Sienna as her coat whips in the wind. "Some people are threatened by other people's powers."

"Willow is threatened by you?"

"Possibly. You see, we live in close proximity and our practices are very different."

"What do you mean by very different?"

"Willow profits from her practice. I happen to believe that's wrong."

"Oh."

Sienna reaches out and puts her hand on my arm. "Just be careful, okay?"

"Of course."

"See you in ballet class," she says with a sad little smile.

I wave to her as I run against the wind and go back into the house. But once I'm inside, her warning seems to reverberate through me, and I wonder if I really want to stay in this place. I mean, I suppose I've learned some helpful things, when I was paying attention, but mostly I feel frustrated and tired, not to mention confused. And the thought of another night of being awakened in the wee hours by my possessed roommate is rather unnerving.

And so, as everyone else is heading to the dining room for a buffet lunch, I decide to make a fast break. I write Caroline a short note, which I put on her pillow, then quickly pack my stuff and make a quiet exit. I feel sort of bad when I consider how I've wasted Dad and Augustine's money, but I also know that I can't stand to stay here through another meal, not to mention another night. And that stupid argument between Sienna and Willow just seemed to seal everything for me. What was up with that little scene anyway? Shouldn't we, the keepers of the power, be able to get along better than that?

As I drive home, I feel lonely and confused. More than ever, I'm missing my mom. I'm wishing I could talk to her, ask her what she thinks about all this. I remember how Sienna made contact with her a couple weeks ago, and I replay the things that Mom said to me through her. Most of them made sense, except for that warning. I still don't get that. But suddenly I'm thinking that maybe it had to do with Willow, sort of like the way Sienna was warning me earlier. Maybe Sienna knows more than she's saying. Maybe I should be careful of Willow. And when I think of how much money I've spent at her shop and then for this seminar, which as it turns out was a waste, well, I can't help but wonder about Willow's motives here. It doesn't really make sense that someone profits from this—like magic is for sale. How can that be right? And how can I ever figure this all out?

# fifteen

On my way home, I stop by Yaquina Lake. I'm not even sure why exactly, maybe just because things seem to be heating up over this development lately. Or maybe it's because I'm still slightly obsessed over this thing with Liz and her parents running roughshod over everyone. Or maybe I simply hope that perhaps my mom's spirit might be hanging out here. Maybe I can make contact with her and she will set me straight on the meaning of the universe.

But when I park the car in the deserted parking lot, I feel like an intruder. And when I get out of the car, it's clear that the wind is picking up and dark clouds are rolling in, and I'm sure there must be a storm on the way. Even so, I stand on the dock, looking out over the steely gray lake as gusts ripple the water, and I long for my mother to speak to me. I try to remember how Marie tilted her head back just so, closing her eyes and focusing. With wind whipping my hair against my cheeks, I try to do the same. I try to center myself, to empty myself, to wait for something to come—to fill me and answer my questions.

And suddenly, to my complete surprise, I feel a presence. But it's not warm and comforting like I'd expect my mom to be. This is cold and icy and harsh, and the impression I'm getting is to throw myself into the lake. Over and over I get this feeling that I should plunge into the lake and simply be done with it. *"Give up. Give up. Give up."*

I snap out of it with a gasp, and the cold air is like a knife in my throat. Then, with trembling knees, I back away from the water, then turn and run straight for my car. Fumbling with the key to unlock the door, I finally get inside and attempt to suppress the voice that continues to tell me, *"Give up!"*

As I drive, I turn on the radio, cranking up KRNK until it finally drowns out the sound of the voice.

# sixteen

I PREPARE MYSELF FOR AUGUSTINE'S QUESTIONS AS I DRIVE INTO TOWN. I'M thinking maybe I should concoct some story as to why I came home early. But, really, I tell myself as I turn down my street, why should I even care what anyone thinks? It is, after all, my life. I'll simply tell Augustine the truth. If the story of my possessed roommate doesn't inspire some sympathy, what difference does it make? Hopefully Dad will understand.

I notice a blue BMW in the driveway and try to remember where I've seen this sporty little car before, and then it hits me that it belongs to Augustine's artist friend Jonathon. Well, he might be the perfect reason for me not to explain too much. I'll simply say hey, then head up to my room without explaining a thing. And then I'll take a nice long nap. But when I go inside, I don't see them. The kitchen is pretty messy with glasses and food plates here and there, almost like someone had a party. I peek into Augustine's studio, but it's quiet and dark with the shades still pulled. Still, I did see her car in the garage, so I know she must be here. Maybe they're outside, although the weather's not too inviting.

I quietly head on upstairs, thinking I'll just avoid them completely as I duck into my room unseen. But before I get to my door, I hear sounds coming from the master bedroom down the hall.

I pause and listen. At first I can't believe what I'm hearing, and it doesn't take a genius to guess what's going on in there. Even so, I am totally stunned. How can this possibly be? How would Augustine dare to do something like this? And in our house? I head straight for the master bedroom door, thinking I'll barge in and confront them, catch them in the act. But then I stop with my fist raised in midair. Seriously, what would I say? And how embarrassing would it be for everyone? Maybe most of all me. I lower my fist and take in a deep breath.

Then I just stand there for a few seconds, listening to what sounds like a steamy scene from a sleazy movie. I'm so astounded that this is happening right here in my own house. And I can't imagine how this is going to hurt my dad. He went for several years without dating, and I really didn't think he'd ever get seriously involved with anyone, and then along came Augustine. I couldn't believe it when they actually connected online. I mean, I'd just assumed the online matchmaker thing might be a good distraction for my dad, a way to get him back into the conversation at least. But then they kept writing each other, and they seemed to really hit it off when they met last winter. After that, it all happened so fast, but Dad seemed so sure, so happy, like a new man.

And now this. I feel sick.

I back up and tiptoe down the hall and into my room, silently closing then locking the door. I set my bag down, then fall across my bed. I want to cry, but it feels like the tears are stuck deep inside me. It feels like everything in me is stuck. And then those words hit me again, *"Give up. Give up. Give up."* Such a sense of hopelessness, like what's the use? Why keep trying? To my amazement, this is followed by the strongest impulse I've ever had to take my own life. Really, it seems the only answer. Suddenly I can think of numerous ways to do it. Like magic, the possibilities flash through my mind. And yet I know that's crazy. Why would I do something so insane? For a few minutes, I wonder if perhaps I am actually losing my mind. I know it could happen. And it seems perfectly logical that it could happen to me. Still, I've heard that the last person to know she's losing her mind is the one going crazy. That should give me hope, but it doesn't.

If only there was someone I could talk to. In the old days, Lucy would've been a good listener. Oh, sure, she sometimes had canned responses like "just pray about it," or "trust God," or "you need to go to church." But even then I found some comfort in knowing that she cared. And, always, she'd end our talks by saying she was going to be praying for me. I'm half tempted to call her and ask her to pray now. But what would she think? That I'd made another stupid mistake? That, just like giving up being vegan, I was now giving up Wicca? Would she say, "I told you so" or "What took you so long?"

I have to ask myself, do I truly want to give up Wicca? I mean, just because I met some strange people this weekend and some weird things happened, and just because the seminar wasn't all that I'd hoped it would be, does that make everything about it all wrong? Didn't I have some honest breakthroughs before? Why am I so willing to toss it all aside now? Isn't that pretty flaky? Maybe I'm just not trying hard enough. Maybe I need to be tougher, like, when the going gets tough the tough get going. I need to make this work!

So I slip on up to the attic and light some candles and do some centering and focusing exercises. And slowly I feel a small sense of power returning to me. And I tell myself that, yes, it's possible to get control again. The magic is in me. It's right at my fingertips. I just need to reach for it. Let the energy flow, breathe it in, breathe it out.

After a while, I hear the sounds of voices and footsteps downstairs, and then I hear the front door close, and I look out the tiny window in time to see Jonathon ducking into his little blue BMW and pulling quickly away. Like they think they're fooling me. Yeah, right.

I'm furious. No, not just furious, I'm enraged. I'm on fire! I feel like I want to kill Augustine, like I could slice her up into little pieces and bury her in the backyard. But then I realize how stupid that is, not to mention a violation of the Rule of Three. No, that would *not* be good. I take in some steadying breaths, recenter myself, and then, when I think I've got some control, go downstairs. I am ready to confront my cheating stepmother. Maybe I'll tell her to pack her bags. I envision myself throwing her paintings and personal things out into the driveway.

"Oh, Heather," she says in a falsely cheerful voice. "I thought I saw your car out there. What brings you home early?" She leans over to put a dish in the dishwasher.

"Never mind that," I say calmly. "What I want to know is why are you cheating on my dad? And why were you and Jonathon *doing it* in my dad's bedroom?"

She blinks and then turns back to the dishwasher. "That's ridiculous, Heather. You must be imagining things. Furthermore, that's my bedroom too."

"That's not the point," I say a bit too loudly.

She stands up straight now, turning to look me in the eyes. "What *is* the point, Heather?" she asks in a very cold voice.

"The point is you're cheating on my dad, Augustine. And I know it!"

She waves her hand. "You just don't understand, that's not what was—"

"I *do* understand," I shout at her. "You and Jonathon were *doing it* in my dad's bed. How can you deny that?"

"I'm just saying you don't understand everything, Heather." Her voice softens now. "I'd think you were more highly evolved than this. You're not a child. You should know that things aren't always as they seem. Sometimes you have to go beneath the surface to get to the truth of things. Can you understand that?"

"What you and Jonathon were doing wasn't beneath the surface," I tell her. "Well, unless it was beneath the surface of my dad's comforter." I make a disgusted face at her as the reality of this hits me full force again. "You make me so sick!" Then I turn and storm off to my bedroom.

She follows me and even knocks on my door. But it's securely locked and I ignore her. Really, what can she possibly say that will change any of this? Even if she goes on about situational ethics, or even if she managed to convince me that something was wrong with her relationship with my dad, it still wouldn't change how I feel. What she did today was wrong. Pure and simple, it was wrong. Not only was it wrong, but I think it was totally premeditated and calculated on her part. I think she jumped on the possibility of Dad and me being gone on the same weekend. She was so eager to get Dad on board for the seminar to get me out of the house. She did all that just so she and Jonathon could have their little tryst, a secret weekend without anyone knowing. She really does make me sick. I can't believe I've ever trusted her with anything.

I can hear her banging away downstairs, slamming doors as she cleans up the kitchen. What on earth does she have to be angry about? Dad and I are the ones who've been betrayed here. Suddenly I feel trapped in my room. But that seems all wrong. She's the one who's done this horrible thing. Why am I the one in prison?

163

I wish there was somewhere I could go, someone to talk to. I know that Lucy's not an option. And I've pretty much burned my bridge with Liz, not that I'd want to speak to her anyway. I remember Sienna and how hurt she was when Willow said those things to her today. And I still don't get that. Why was Willow being so harsh? Was it like Sienna said? Were they really in some kind of power struggle? And if that's true, wouldn't my allegiance lie with Sienna? I decide to go visit her. Maybe I can encourage her. Maybe she can help me with this new problem.

I wait until it gets quiet on the first floor, then I slip downstairs and out the front door and into my car, driving away as fast as I can and not looking back. I wish I could just keep going and going. Instead, I drive downtown, park at the dance studio, and quietly go up the stairs to Sienna's apartment. But then I hear the sound of piano and I think she must be playing for a class. This surprises me because I thought she had the whole day off to teach at the seminar. But when I stick my head into the dance studio, there she is, plunking away on the piano. She notices me, nodding solemnly, and I just wave and leave. I know that lessons will go until around five. Maybe I can kill time for a couple of hours.

I start to drive up to my favorite beach spot, then realize that the weather is really not compatible to beach walking, and so I head back to town. I drive through town, where it's beginning to rain, finally deciding to go to the WC, where I can get a cup of Chai tea. I'm longing for something, anything, that feels even close to "normal" right now.

I get my tea and go to a table in the back of the room. I still have my Book of Shadows in my bag and I'm thinking I might be able to strengthen myself by reading and writing in it, but when I open it up to the latest spot, I'm taken aback. The handwriting is someone else's. Someone has gotten ahold of my book and written horrible, mean, gross, and vulgar words in it. And there is even some nasty-looking artwork. I feel sickened just looking at it. Who could've done —

"Heather," says a girl's voice. I look up to see Lucy standing in front of me.

I slam the book shut and stare at her.

"Are you okay?" she asks with a creased brow.

My hands are shaking and I feel like I could actually throw up. That's how vile the writing in my book was just now. And I still can't figure out who did it.

"You look like you've seen a ghost," she says, seriously concerned. "Are you okay?"

I consider this. Maybe that's exactly what happened. Maybe I did see a ghost. Of course, I can't say this. Especially not to Lucy. "I'm just upset," I say, pushing the book back into my purse.

"Is that a witch's book?" she asks.

I shrug.

"Can't you see that's your problem?" she says. "That stuff is evil, Heather. It's going to mess you up."

I sit up straighter now. "That's *not* what's messing me up, Lucy," I say in a stiff voice. "Not that you'd care. But, for your information, I have way worse problems to think about right now."

"Like what?" she says with interest.

"What difference does it make?" I just shake my head. "I mean, you'd probably try to pin everything on witchcraft anyway. What's the point in talking about it?"

She actually seems to consider this. "Maybe you're right. I probably would connect your problems to the sin of witchcraft, which is probably totally accurate. But you would simply deny it. So, really,

I guess there isn't any point in talking." Her brows draw together. "Sorry to bother you, Heather."

I shrug. "Seems more like I bothered you."

Then she just walks away. Honestly, I can almost see her shaking the dust off her feet as she goes. Like I might've exposed her to something evil and contagious. Whatever.

I wait until she leaves the WC before I retrieve my Book of Shadows. Something occurred to me when she said it looked like I'd seen a ghost. I got to thinking perhaps a ghost wrote in my book. I do remember writing in it last night, and how the pen raced over the pages, and how I was almost unconscious of what was being written, but how I was so exhausted when I was done. Perhaps a spirit was writing a message through me. So I go back to the words, but once again, I feel assaulted by the words there. And confused by the lack of meaning. I hate to admit it, but it really does seem evil. Perhaps even demonic. I remember Caroline's night terrors. Perhaps we were both attacked by the same spirit. I glance at the clock and see that it's nearly five. I gather my things, go out into the wind and rain, race to my car, and then drive it around the block, where I park it in back. I go upstairs, taking my time as I use the bathroom, slowly washing my hands, waiting for the last song of the day to end. If only my troubles could end as simply as that. The haunting echo of the last note, hanging in the air . . . then gone.

# seventeen

"Sienna," I say with relief when she finally trudges up the stairs to where I'm waiting like a stalker halfway up the stairwell. "I really need to talk."

She nods and continues slowly plodding up as if her legs were made of lead. "I thought so," she says breathlessly when we reach the top.

"My life is falling apart."

"Uh-huh." She removes a key from her sweater pocket. Then she opens the door and waves me inside her apartment.

"I'm so glad you're here," I say as she turns on a light. "I thought maybe you took the whole day off."

"So you left the seminar?"

"Yes." Then I tell her about my roommate's weird nighttime antics and even show her the writing in my book.

She nods. "Yes, this is definitely the work of a bad spirit, Heather."

"A bad spirit?"

"Yes. I know you're a novice, but you need to understand that when you're dealing with the powers of the universe, there are both good and evil. You have to respect both equally."

"But why did the bad spirit write in my book?" I ask.

She closes the book and hands it back to me. "I don't know. Perhaps you have that answer hidden inside of you."

"Was it related to Caroline?" I persist. "I mean, she was saying some pretty nasty stuff last night. It reminded me of some of this."

She shrugs. "It's surprising how uncreative the evil spirits can be. I've seen this exact same thing time and time again."

"Really?"

She nods. "Sad but true. Do you want a cup of tea?"

"Sure." I follow her over to an area that serves as a small kitchen. I sit on a stool by a little table and watch as she fills a teakettle, then turns on the gas. "So is there anything you can do about it? Is there a way to keep the evil spirits away?"

"Some people think that if you focus on good magic, it will keep them at bay. Unfortunately, I can't say that's always true."

"What *is* true?"

"That once you open the door, once they come in, well, sometimes they like to stick around."

"Have you had this problem personally?" I ask.

She doesn't say anything but just keeps digging through a small cupboard as if she's trying to avoid my question. And suddenly I get really scared. I imagine that she, like Caroline, might be possessed by one of those things. I get this picture of her turning around with wriggling black snakes coming out of her eyes, or green puke spewing from her twisted mouth, or maybe her head will spin around a couple of times and she'll come at me with knives. I'm ready to run. But when she turns around she looks perfectly normal. "Herbal or black?"

"Huh?"

"What kind of tea?" She holds two boxes up.

"Herbal is fine."

She putters around and finally hands me a cup of tea and we go back to sit in the living room area. "Yes," she says as she blows steam from her black tea. "I've had my own struggles with evil spirits too. Unfortunately, I think that's one of the untold stories of the craft."

"Why is that?" I ask. "I mean, can't you use your good power against the bad spirits?"

"Sometimes you can. But sometimes their power is stronger. It's very complicated, Heather. If I knew all the answers, I suppose I'd be running the universe. As it is, I'm still a student myself."

"But Willow hired you to teach this weekend."

She nods. "Yes, a mutual friend—one who wasn't that sure about Willow—told her about me. You see, in some circles I'm fairly well known and even respected."

"But not by Willow?"

"Willow and I don't agree on everything. And I suppose it didn't help matters when I met her this morning before my workshop and questioned why she was peddling all her wares at the seminar. To profit like that, well, it seems wrong to me."

"Oh."

"Yes, I offended her."

"I thought it was just a power struggle."

She nods. "Oh, there's that too. I think that Willow and I are simply not well aligned in the constellations. You meet some people like that. It's best to avoid them." She looks directly at me now. "Like your friend Liz. Or should I say ex-friend? Do you want to tell me what happened between you and her? Last time we talked, it wasn't so good. But seeing you girls at ballet, it seems to have gotten even worse. It's as if an invisible wall of ice has been erected between you two."

So I confess to Sienna about my spell.

"You got something like that from Willow?" she practically explodes. "That's inexcusable and I'll—"

"No, no . . . I got it from a girl I met at Willow's shop. Her name is Jane. She put it together for me and told me what to do. I paid her for it."

"Oh, Heather." Sienna shakes her head with dismay. "You should know better."

"I know."

"The Rule of Three."

I look up at her and nod. "Yes, and I'm sure I've had more than three times come back on me." Then I tell her all about Augustine and Jonathon and how I surprised them by coming home early today.

Sienna almost laughs. "You actually walked in on them?"

"Well, not actually. They were in my dad's bedroom with the door closed, but that didn't hide the obvious."

"Too bad."

"I'll say." I set my cup down. "I feel so sorry for Dad. I mean, he never dated after Mom died. I really didn't think he'd ever remarry. In some ways I feel like it's my fault."

"Your fault?"

"I'm the one who originally got my dad to try the online match-making service. I only suggested it because it seemed like he was in a slump. I figured it couldn't hurt. I never dreamed they'd get married."

"Was your dad in love?"

"I think so. Actually, I thought he was more enchanted at first. I mean, Augustine is, well, she's one of those people who can captivate almost anyone. You should know, you've met her. She's so unique and talented, and she can talk about anything. I actually wondered if she was into witchcraft at first," I admit. "I thought maybe she'd charmed him or something."

"But she's not?"

"Not really. She's into eclecticism or something like that."

"Meaning she picks and chooses. A spirituality smorgasbord."

"Yeah, that sounds about right."

"So what are you going to do?"

"About what?" I ask.

"About Augustine and your dad."

I think about this. "What should I do? I mean, at first I was ready to call Dad and tell him the whole thing. But then I realized how much it would hurt him. And he's right in the middle of this case. What should I do?"

She just shakes her head. "I don't know, but—"

"But the answer is in me," I finish for her.

She smiles. "You're learning."

"But what if the answer's *not* in me? What if I'm just going to go around in circles getting more and more lost?" I almost tell her about the impression I've had to just give up . . . *completely*. But I think I'm ashamed. It sounds so weak, so flaky. I hate being flaky.

"I think you'll find the answer, Heather. Eventually."

My tea is gone now, and so, it seems, is Sienna's advice. Not that she really had much. But at least she listened. That was something. "I guess I should go," I say.

She nods. "Yes. I actually have a dinner thing tonight."

For some reason this surprises me. I guess I assumed that she had no social life, no friends. Apparently I got her confused with me.

"Take care, Heather." Then before I go out the door, she holds up both hands. "Maybe that was it!" she says suddenly. "Maybe

171

that's what your mother's warning was about. Remember the family member who was going to hurt you?"

"You think it's Augustine?"

"What do you think?"

I consider this as I go out. It has to be Augustine. Of course, how could anyone hurt me more than she has by doing this? As I drive home, it occurs to me that the things with Liz, which seemed enormous a week ago, have suddenly diminished compared to what is now happening between Augustine and my dad. Poor Dad. I have no idea how he's going to take this. But I know I'll be there for him. He's going to need me more than ever now.

Augustine and I both avoid each other for the rest of the evening and into the next day. I think we're both laying low until Dad gets home. Although I have no idea what her plan is or how this will play out, I am determined to be honest for Dad's sake. And I'll be there for him. Maybe we will throw Augustine out together. Send the tramp packing. She deserves it.

But Sunday stretches into the evening and I realize that not only has Dad not come home, but Augustine's car is gone. Still, this may be good news. Maybe he's just delayed and she got nervous and decided to make a fast break. Maybe she left him a note. But I snoop around, even going into the master bedroom, where I see that her clothes and things are still here. And no note.

Dad and Augustine finally arrive around nine, pulling into the driveway almost simultaneously. I go into the kitchen to wait for them, ready for the big confrontation. But before I have a chance to say a word, Dad begins to speak.

"Augustine has told me the whole story," he says calmly when he sees me. "She's very sorry that you've misunderstood things, Heather. But I'm disappointed to hear how you made such snap judgments against her. That doesn't sound like you."

"But did she tell you about Jonathon?" I demand.

He nods. "Yes, she told me everything."

"And you're okay with that?"

"I understand how it might appear, Heather. And I know why you're having such a hard time with it. It's not easy having a step-mom, and these things are apt to happen. But sometimes you have to forgive and forget. Let bygones be bygones. Are you able to do that?"

I stare at my dad as if he's an alien. Maybe he is. How is it that he's okay with this? It's too weird.

"I'm sorry," I tell him. Then I turn and glare at Augustine. "But I'm not okay with this. I think Augustine is a horrible person and I wish she'd just leave."

"Heather!" says Dad, his eyes angry.

"I can't believe you'd take her side!" I yell. "She's nothing but a—"

"That's enough!" He points his finger toward the stairs. "If you can't treat Augustine with more respect than that, you are excused."

"You can't just *excuse* me, Dad!" I scream. "I'm not eight years old, you know. I live here too. This is my house. And if you're going to allow Augustine to turn it into—"

"HEATHER!" my dad yells, getting my attention. This is a man who *never* raises his voice. "Get out of here!"

I can't believe it. My dad is losing his mind. Maybe Augustine really does practice witchcraft. Maybe she's on the evil side and plans to destroy both of us. I just stand there staring at both of them, too angry to speak, too shocked to move.

"You are excused," says my dad in a calmer tone. "Until you can come down and apologize to your stepmother. Thank you."

I turn and head for the garage, thinking I'll jump in my car and run away from here. Who needs them? Who needs this? But Dad steps in front of me. "You aren't going anywhere in the car tonight, Heather. You can go to your room. Think about what you've said to Augustine and to me. If you want to come down and act like a civilized—"

"Why should I act civilized?" I yell, turning and heading toward the stairs. "You people are total barbarians!"

I hear my dad saying something that sounds apologetic to Augustine, like he's worried about *her* feelings. Then, as I stomp up the stairs, I hear her answer him in a soothing tone, saying he shouldn't blame himself for my actions. Like this is all my fault, like she's the victim here. Give me a break!

I've never wanted to run away from home before, never saw the sense in trying to escape your problems. But I do now. I am like so outta here! And so I begin to plot out how I will do this thing—the great escape. At first I think I'll leave tonight, maybe wait until they go to bed. But then I realize that's too risky. If I'm noticed, I know that Dad would probably call the police. I'd probably get picked up and end up in more trouble than ever.

So I decide I will wait until tomorrow. I'll pretend to go to school in the morning, but I'll just keep driving. I don't know where I'll go, but anywhere would be better than here. Anything would be better than this. I hate them both! I hate this whole town. I hate my life!

# eighteen

AT FIRST I ASSUME THAT IT'S MY ANGER KEEPING ME AWAKE. AND WHY should that surprise me, since I'm still feeling enraged and it's past midnight? But finally I tell myself to just chill, that I need a good night's rest if I'm going to make a break for it in the morning. But then I realize it's something more that's bothering me. It's like I can feel a presence in my room. A very real and *unearthly* presence. At first I hope that it's my mom's spirit, coming to comfort me, to help me. And I actually address this spirit. I whisper into the darkness, "I know you're here. I can feel you, but I don't know who you are. Please, reveal yourself to me." But that doesn't work. Then I think maybe Oliver has sneaked in here; he can be a real prowler at night. So I turn on the light and look around, but he's not here. I turn off the light and take in several soothing deep breaths. I'm probably just having a case of nerves.

And then, just when I start to relax, I get this very cold and menacing feeling, almost as if someone, rather a spirit, has just blown his icy breath over me. This is definitely not my mother. There's no way she would make me feel this scared. It's obvious that this is a dark spirit. Perhaps the same one that had been troubling Caroline, the one who wrote in my Book of Shadows. Part of me is tempted to speak to this apparition again, to muster bravery and try to see what's troubling him. Perhaps I can help. But it's like I'm frozen and unable to do anything but lie here like a stiff board.

I don't know what to do with this kind of paralyzing fear. It's unlike anything I've ever felt before. And I don't know how to get rid of it. So I just close my eyes tightly, pretending I'm asleep, and focus my will to wish it away. I think words like "depart" and "you are vanquished." But I'm unable to say the words aloud. It feels like I may never be able to speak again. It's even getting hard to breathe.

My energy feels useless against this thing. It's obvious that my power is nothing compared to its force. Whatever it is lingers here, growing like an ominous black cloud that invades and fills every cubic inch of my room. I think perhaps this presence is toxic, too. Even the air feels lethal. Maybe this horrible being plans to kill me before morning. And maybe that would be a relief. Or perhaps I will simply succumb to terror in the night and quit breathing altogether. Isn't it possible to be literally scared to death? I can feel my heart rate accelerating, my breathing getting labored. It feels as if someone has placed a heavy bag of stones upon my chest, crushing the air and the life out of me. And I am giving in to it.

Time passes and I realize that somehow I must've managed to sleep. Or maybe I passed out from fear. But I'm wide awake now. And although it's barely dawn, I get up and put the things together that I think I will need for my escape. To avoid suspicion, I will only use my backpack, but I pack it carefully with warm clothes and socks, rolling them so they will fit. Then I layer some clothes on myself as well, topping this with my parka. I look a little chubby, but I'm guessing no one will notice. Why would they? As it turns out, my dad has already left for the office, and although I can hear Augustine in her studio, she doesn't come out when I tiptoe through the kitchen, pausing to grab a bottle of juice from the fridge. I'm sure she's not eager to speak to me this morning. Perhaps she's still playing the wounded victim. What do I care? I slip out and get into my car and off I go.

Just for effect, I turn down the street toward the school, but then I just keep driving without looking back. And soon I'm on the highway, heading north. Maybe I'll go to Canada. I'm not sure. But anywhere is better than here. Let them have each other. Maybe they're both cheating on each other, both having affairs. Maybe they'll feel more free now, able to do as they like after I'm gone. Perhaps they'll invite all their lovers over and have orgies right there in our house—in the living room even. I do *not* even care! I don't! I really, really don't! I hate them. I hate them both! They deserve each other!

But even as I think these bitter thoughts, I can feel my eyes filling with hot tears. And then they slip soundlessly down my cheeks. *Don't pay attention to this,* I tell myself. I can't possibly be crying for Augustine and Dad. They're not worth it. They don't even care.

Soon I'm coming up to the lighthouse, the same place where the seminar was just held during the weekend. Of course, everyone is gone now. Probably since midday yesterday. For no explainable reason, well, other than to dry my face, I pull over, going into the viewpoint parking lot. And then I turn off my car and just sit there. I am so lost. Lost and miserable. And lonely. I remember that divining card that Willow gave me the first day I visited her shop. I remember how she pulled out the Heather card, and she didn't even know my name. But the warning on the card was that I could become isolated, lonely, in despair. Well, that certainly was prophetic.

And then, almost as if someone has whispered the answer into my ear, I know exactly what I'm going to do. It's plain and clear and simple. And it makes perfect sense. Almost as if someone or something has taken my hand, I feel this presence guiding me. I remove the keys from the ignition and slip them into in my backpack, which I leave on the passenger seat. I won't even lock the doors. Why make this difficult for whoever figures this out later today, or perhaps tomorrow? Maybe they will say, "Wasn't that thoughtful of her to leave the keys behind and the car unlocked like that?" It will make it much easier to move the car from here after I'm gone.

Then I get out of the car and walk over to the viewpoint area along the edge of the parking lot. Normally the view is spectacular from this spot. Tourists stop here to take photos all the time. The lighthouse and keeper's house is picturesque, off the right, and then there's nothing but ocean as far as the eye can see, which isn't far today since it's foggy and gray. "Pea soup," my mom used to say to describe days like this. Funny I should think of that just now. Then it occurs to me that perhaps Mom is the one here with me right now. Maybe she is my guide. I've read about spirit guides. Perhaps she is the one holding my hand, lovingly leading me like this. Showing me the end to my trouble. I feel so calm. So at peace. And yet it's cold out here. The air seems to seep right through all the layers of clothes. But soon it will be over.

I go up to the wall of stone and look over the edge. The drop-off must be at least a hundred feet. Maybe more. I've never been good at estimating distances. But I do know that it's straight down. I can see that much. At the bottom are jagged rocks and pounding surf. No possible way to survive a fall like this.

I climb up on the rock ledge and stand there looking down. It makes me dizzy and I can feel myself swaying slightly, to and fro, and I know that a gust of wind could end this thing—for good. I'm not sure how long I stand there or why I don't just lean forward and plunge down, but suddenly, like someone has thrown a bucket of water over my head, I realize what I'm about to do.

I step back, almost losing my balance, and then I partially jump, partially fall, back onto the asphalt parking lot. I lean against the wall, clutching my hands to my chest as my heart pounds so hard that I wonder if I might actually die from a heart attack. What just happened? I look around, almost as if I expect to see someone—someone who intervened. Someone who wanted to get my attention. But there is no one here. At least no one I can see.

My legs feel weak, like noodles, as I walk back to the car. And then I'm assaulted with a barrage of negative thoughts. It feels as if someone is throwing stones at me. Telling me that I'm such a loser, such a failure. What's wrong with me that I couldn't even complete something as simple as this? It should've been so easy. Why didn't I go through with it? Can't I do anything right? I am hopeless, pathetic, a wimp, a fool. I am not worthy to inhabit the earth, the universe, or even my own death. I will never fit in. "Give up!"

And yet as I get into the car, there is this tiny sense of relief—just the faintest whisper of something. Could it be hope? That seems unlikely. But there is something. I tell myself that even if I am wrong, even if I couldn't jump just now, it doesn't mean that I won't later. I probably just needed to plan this thing better. Perhaps there's something I forgot to do first. *Like what?* I wonder as I lean my head against the steering wheel. *Like what?*

Of course, it comes to me now! I need to write a suicide letter so that they will know this wasn't an accident, or a murder, or a mistake. I should write a note that's so explicit that everyone will feel guilty. Not only Dad and Augustine, but Hudson and Liz and even Lucy. People should know how deeply they've hurt me. And, yes, especially Dad. Of all the wounds I've received lately, his is by far the deepest, the deadliest, the absolute worst! He deserves to know this.

So I open my backpack in search of paper. But my school things aren't in here. And, in my haste to pack so many clothes, I didn't even bring my Book of Shadows. I cannot find the tiniest scrap of paper. I search in the glove box and unearth an old pen, which may or may not work, but other than a plastic-coated insurance card and the dog-eared car manual, there is nothing I can really write on.

I begin to search the car for something, even if it's just an old fast-food napkin. But I thoroughly cleaned my car last Friday in anticipation of the weekend seminar. There is nothing there except the old plaid blanket that Mom put in the car years ago. Maybe under the seat. I never clean under the seats. Out of sight, out of mind. So I actually get out of the car and onto my knees to dig beneath the driver's seat. To my surprise, my hands touch something that feels like a small spiral notebook. Perfect! I pull it out and wipe the dust and grime from the dark cover, then open it only to discover that it's already been written in. It's completely filled with writing. My mother's handwriting. Page after page of words! My mother's words!

This is incredible. I can't believe I've never found it before. I turn back to the first page and begin to read.

*The treatments are not working. Not the chemo, not the radiation. Nothing can stop this hideous invader named Cancer. It has taken over my body. I will be dead within the year. This is so unfair—so wrong. I should be in the prime of my life. My daughter will be a teenager soon. And she will have no mother to guide her. Oh, God, why have you done this to me?*

Suddenly I remember how my mother used to write in this small black notebook when she was sick. She called it her thinking book, but she would never let me read it. And whenever I walked in to find her writing, she would close it and quickly tuck it away as if it contained deep, dark secrets, things I was too young to understand. I turn the page and read on, and I cry as I come to places where my mother sounds so totally depressed, so sad, so lost and desperate and ready to give up. Exactly how I feel today. There is comfort here. And I think this is no coincidence that I found this book. I think that Mom really was guiding me. I think that she wanted me to know this—everything about her—before I take the big plunge. I think she really was holding my hand.

After a couple of hours, I realize that I'm freezing cold. Despite my layers of clothes, the cold damp air has seeped into the car and I'm shivering. I turn on the ignition and the heater and continue to read. I feel that Mom is here right now, sitting right next to me in the passenger's seat, saying, "Go on, read it all, Heather. The answer to life is here."

> *I used to believe in God. I used to think that he was the giver of life, the creator of everything, a loving and benevolent God. But I do not believe that now. If God is real, I believe he is cruel, sadistic, a torturer with a wicked sense of humor. And if he has the answers, I believe he is keeping them to himself, wearing his poker face, and playing his cards close to his chest.*

*Yes,* I think, *I agree with you, Mom.* That is exactly how I feel too. I can't believe we are so much alike. I can't believe I almost died without knowing this. It will be such a comfort to me now, when I stand back on that rock ledge, to know that my own mother knew just exactly how I felt. I imagine her standing there with me, holding my hand as together we both jump.

I continue to read, almost growing impatient with this delay in doing what I know I must do. I'm halfway tempted to set the book aside right now. Maybe I should just go out there and finish what I've started and have Mom fill me in on all the details afterward, since I'm sure we'll be together soon. But for whatever reason, I feel that I should read to the end. It seems only right.

My mother dated all her entries, and I can tell by the dates that the time of her death is only about a couple of weeks away. And yet she still seems so sad and lonely, so lost and confused and frustrated. She keeps asking the same questions about God and life and death and the universe, probing deeper and deeper each time, but she never gets any real answers. It's breaking my heart. And I'm getting angry too. It was all so unfair. So wrong. I can't believe how well she concealed her pain and heartache from me during that time. She always seemed so strong, so reserved, so confident. I can't believe it was all just an act. And yet I know that it helped me get through it. Maybe that's just what mothers do. Maybe I'll never fully understand any of this.

*Vince said not to, but I'm taking a road trip anyway. I know that I can't put it off another day. By next week I may be too weak to drive. As much as I hate leaving Heather behind, even for a couple of days, I know this is something I must do. I'm doing it for me.*

I look back at the date and realize this must be the time she went to visit an old school friend. I can't remember the woman's name, but I do remember being a little miffed that Mom was going away for the weekend and that she refused to take me with her. I thought that was very selfish. It shames me to think that I even threw a little hissy fit over the whole thing. Poor Mom. I read on about how she will drive to Seal Rock and spend a couple of days with Diane. Oh, yes, I remember now, the woman's name was Diane Ross. Sort of like that singer only it was Diane, not Diana. I remember how, when I was little, I thought Mom actually did go to school with Diana Ross and how I wanted to meet this famous woman. But Mom has assured me they were not the same.

> Although the drive is only two hours, I must take a break midway. I need to rest. And I need to write. I need to sort out my feelings about my old friend. I used to envy her. She seemed to have such wisdom and understanding, so at peace with God and life. Even when her mother died during our first year in high school, Diane handled it with incredible grace. I was amazed. And since then, Diane has been no stranger to trials. A few years ago, her husband left her with two little boys to raise, and yet Diane manages it. She is the most grounded woman I've ever known. I so wish I could be like her. I wish that she could tell me her secrets. I know she's religious. But that was something she learned from her family. Simply the way she was raised. Going to church for them was like going to the grocery store. It was something they just did without questioning it. A

*way of life. Even when I went with her sometimes, I still couldn't grasp the whole thing. I thought it was slightly archaic, silly even, not to mention boring. Oh, I never told my friend any of this. Just like I'm not telling her everything right now. Poor Diane has no idea how advanced my cancer is. I'm sure she would never have invited me for the weekend if she knew. She would have insisted on coming to see me. But that just wouldn't work. Diane thinks we are going to go places and see things. She even mentioned a girls' night out. When I arrive I will have to explain myself.*

I eagerly turn the page as if I'm reading a gripping novel. I can't wait to hear how this visit goes with Diane. And I do remember my mom seeming different after she came home, after her visit. I assumed it was because Diane was so much fun. Then, just days later, Mom's health went downhill. Dad blamed it on the road trip. She was bedridden and died the following week. It all seemed to happen so fast. Even though we'd known it was coming, we weren't prepared for it. We weren't ready to let her go. I turn the page. I can tell this is the last entry, but at least it's fairly long. My hands begin to tremble as I read the words.

*So much to think about . . . so much to write . . . I don't quite know where to begin. I am on my way home again. And, oh, I am so eager to get back. It feels as if it's been two years instead of two days. I need to see my Heather. I need to stroke that beautiful brown hair again, to feel her nestling in my* arms. And I need to see Vince. I have so much to tell him. I wonder if he will understand. I'm not even sure that I understand all of the ramifications. At least not with my head. I understand with my heart. It's as if God turned on a lightbulb and suddenly things began to make sense. "Faith is a gift from God," Diane told me. "You can't muster it up yourself, Lily. But if you ask him, he will give it to you." Then she went on to explain how God never promised us a perfect life here on earth, but that he promised to walk with us through the hard things, to help us, to love us, to forgive us, and to strengthen us. "But you have to allow him," she told me. "He won't force his way onto you. He wants you to surrender to him, Lily. You must trust him with every bit of your life, you must invite him into your heart, and then it will all begin to make sense." And so, sitting there in her sunny yellow breakfast room, I allowed Diane to lead me in a prayer. I invited God to come into my heart. Actually, I invited his Son, Jesus, whom Diane assured me is one and the same as God Almighty. I don't claim to understand all this yet. But I do know what happened in my heart when I did this yesterday. It was as if a huge weight was lifted from me. And it was replaced with the greatest sense of peace I've ever known. And, to my utter surprise, this was followed with a real joy. Not that sort of jumping-up-and down childish joy, it's much deeper than that. I am so tired. I will rest and pray. Hopefully I will make it the rest of the way home.

*With God's help, I will. And I will tell my family about this. I hope they can understand. God can help them understand. This is my earnest prayer. Dear, loving God, you must take care of Vince and Heather for me. You must watch over them. You must help them find their own way to you. So that we can one day meet again. Amen.*

That's it. No more words, nothing, just several blank pages. Enough for me to write a long suicide note. But now I'm not so sure. Somehow I don't think that's what Mom had in mind for me after all. Sitting there in my idling car, a memory hits me. I recall how she talked about God after her visit with Diane. I remember how her eyes lit up, how she said, "God is so miraculous." I thought she meant she was going to get well. I thought when she said, "Things have changed," it meant that she'd been healed of her cancer. I also remember how she encouraged me to go to church, to go and find my own answers. That's probably the reason I became friends with Lucy. Still, it never made sense. It doesn't make sense now. I feel bewildered, like I was driving along and missed the turn. I am more lost than ever.

# nineteen

I CALL INFORMATION AND ASK FOR THE NUMBER OF DIANE ROSS IN SEAL ROCK. I have no idea if she still lives there, but I think it's worth a shot. And then my call is put through, which makes me think I'm on the right track, but I get an answering machine. I listen to the message. The voice is warm and welcoming, but instead of leaving a message, I hang up, start the car, and drive north.

It's past noon when I get to Seal Rock. And to my surprise, I feel ravenous, so I stop at a small greasy-looking café. I thought I'd given up red meat, but feeling like I've been wrong about so many things, and possibly as a way to thumb my nose at Augustine, I order a cheeseburger with everything. It tastes like the best thing I've ever eaten. Then, after I'm done, I go across the street to a phone booth by a gas station and look up Diane Ross's name. To my relief, it's listed, along with a street address. I ask the attendant for directions, then drive around the small town until I find an old-fashioned cottage-style house with gray shingle siding and bright red trim. I park in front and just sit there. I suspect that no one's home, but I figure I should probably go up and knock. Still, I have no idea what I'll say if someone opens the door.

I think I'm relieved when no one answers. Not that I'm leaving. My plan is to sit here until Diane comes home. Hopefully the neighbors won't think I'm a stalker. I study her house. I like the little front porch with its two wicker rockers. It looks like a nice place to chat and drink lemonade. If it were warmer, that is. I can't believe I've never met this woman before. Judging by her house, I think I'd like her. But then maybe I have met her. Now that I think of it, there were a lot of people I'd never seen before at Mom's funeral. I suppose I was too distracted to really notice.

As I wait for her to come home, I reread some pages of my mom's journal. The words sound so much like her and make me feel close to her, as if she really is speaking to me. And I carefully reread that last section, still trying to put it all together. It's plain to see that something huge happened to her while visiting Diane, but it irks me to know that she never really got a chance to tell us much about it. She was gone so quickly afterward.

A white car pulls into the driveway. I sort of jump, then prepare myself for whatever is coming next. Not that I exactly know how to do that. But I take in a slow, deep breath, trying to steady myself as I see a tall woman getting out of the car. She's looking curiously over at my car. So, still holding on to Mom's journal like it's my lifeline, I get out of my car and call to her. "Diane?"

She nods. "Yes?"

"Diane Ross?"

Again, she nods. "Yes. Can I help you?"

I approach her. "My name is Heather Sinclair," I begin.

She smiles now, quickly walking toward me with her hand outstretched. "Heather! Lily's daughter. Why, I haven't seen you in years. You're all grown-up now."

I sort of shrug. "I'm sixteen."

"How *are* you?" she asks, peering into my eyes as if she's really looking at me, as if she really wants to know how I am, instead of just being courteous.

"I'm not sure." I glance over my shoulder. I guess I'm having second thoughts, feeling nervous, maybe I should just run.

"Well, come inside," she says, placing a hand on my shoulder and guiding me up the front walk. "I'm ready for a cup of tea. It's been so chilly today."

So we go into her house, which is just as charming on the inside as the outside, and soon she's putting on a kettle and just chattering away at me as if I'm a long-lost friend.

"I was showing a house just now," she says. "I'm a real-estate agent. Anyway, it's so foggy and cold that I don't think the prospective buyers were very impressed. It's always so much easier to sell houses on sunny days." She laughs as she fills a teapot with hot water. "But I'm sure you didn't come all this way to hear about that." She opens a box of chocolate-mint cookies and arranges some in a neat circle on a pretty porcelain plate. "Want to take these over to the breakfast nook?" she says. "There's a heater vent underneath the table, and it's always warm and cozy. I'll bring our tea."

So I take the plate of cookies and scoot onto the padded bench seat. I notice that the walls are, indeed, a sunny yellow like my mom described. And even on this gray day, I find this space comforting.

Her porcelain teapot is painted with delicate purple violets. She brings it over on a tray, then carefully fills up some very dainty matching teacups. "I always think that tea tastes better in china cups," she says as she hands me a cup and saucer. "Just something my grandmother taught me."

I smell the tea, which isn't herbal, but for some reason it seems familiar. "I know this is a black tea," I say, "but what kind is it?"

"I'm sorry, I should've warned you. It's Earl Grey, the only kind I drink."

189

"My mother only drank herbal tea," I say. "Well, after she got sick anyway. She used to drink another kind of tea before that. Maybe it was Earl Grey."

"I find the aroma comforting," she says. "It reminds me of lavender and sunshine."

I nod. "Yes. That's what it smells like." Suddenly I realize that I really don't like herbal tea. I only drank it because of my mom, and then later because of Augustine. This is much better. Go figure.

She makes a bit more small talk, then finally asks. "I'm so curious as to why you came to see me, Heather. Although I'm very pleased that you did. Are you going to tell me what brings you here?"

"Do you want the long version or the nutshell?" I ask.

She smiles. "I have all the time in the world."

At first I think I'll only tell her some things. Not everything. I'm afraid the whole truth would be too shocking. And yet something about this woman, or maybe the things my mom wrote about her, tells me maybe she can handle it. And so I spill my entire story. Starting with witchcraft and bad spells and Liz and Hudson and finally ending with Augustine's affair and my father's betrayal, and even my unsuccessful attempt at suicide.

"My goodness," she says when I finally finish. "You've had quite a time of it, haven't you, Heather?"

I hold up Mom's journal now. "I just found this today," I explain. "It must've been underneath the driver's seat ever since my mom came here to see you, right before she died. It's the only thing that kept me from another attempt at jumping off the cliff." Then I tell her about the last entry. "That's why I came to see you."

She pours us both another cup of tea. "I'm so glad you did, Heather. I think this must've been a divine appointment."

"A what?"

"I think God arranged for you to come here today." She shakes her head slowly. "You see, I was supposed to be on a fall-foliage trip right now. My sister and I set it up last year. We were going to spend two weeks driving over to the East Coast, visiting states like Vermont and Connecticut to see the autumn leaves and historical sites. But her husband got very sick and we had to cancel. And so here I am at home, ready for you to come and visit. I believe God set that up, in the same way he worked it out for your mother to come here. I had no idea when she came that her cancer was so advanced. I was stunned when she died so soon afterward. But I was also thankful. That too had been a divine appointment." She smiles at me. "God really does know what he's doing. And right now, he's trying to get your attention, Heather."

"How can you be so sure?" I ask.

"It comes from a lifetime of knowing him in my heart," she says. "And reading the Bible and praying. Just the basics of belief. God has all the answers."

"I'm not so sure about that," I say. "I mean, what about witchcraft? I feel like I've found some answers in that. And it's definitely real. I saw and experienced supernatural things that I know were for real. How can I be sure that's not the answer I need?"

She smiles. "Is it working for you?"

I shrug. "Maybe not too well. But it's still a real thing."

"Of course it's a real thing, Heather. There are lots of spiritual forces in the world. There's no denying that the supernatural exists. But just because it exists doesn't mean that it's more powerful than God. That's like comparing a firefly to the sun."

"Even so, how can I know that God is right for me? Simply because he's more powerful?"

"God is the highest spiritual force there is. He is the Creator, the

Supreme Power, and King of the Universe. And one day all spiritual forces, including everything associated with witchcraft, will
bow down and acknowledge that he is Lord of all and that they are
powerless before him. He is that huge, that powerful, and yet he
loves you so much he was willing to set it all aside just to reach you.
His greatest desire is to enter into a personal and loving relationship
with you."

Now, I can't explain how or why, but when Diane says this, something in me sort of clicks. Like, *I know*. Like, *This is the truth*. Still, I
don't want to seem so easily swayed. I've made so many quick deci-
sions about important things lately, and so often I've been wrong.
What if I'm wrong now?

"I know a little about witchcraft," she says.

For some reason this surprises me. I'm sure my jaw drops as I
wait for her to explain.

"My sister got into it when she was in college. We'd been raised
as Christians, and I think she just wanted to rebel. Consequently she
started dabbling in witchcraft. Fortunately, that only lasted about a
year for her. She got so depressed and confused that she knew it was
wrong. She'd experienced enough of the Lord to know the difference between a life filled with things like hope, love, forgiveness,
joy, mercy, and how it compared with living in darkness and fear
and doubt. And do you know what she told me when she gave it
up?"

"No."

"Well, she actually said a lot of things . . . for instance, how
instead of feeling powerful, she began to feel very fearful."

"I know that feeling."

"She told me how evil spirits had plagued her, and how she'd
learned that was the reason the Bible was so clear in its warnings

against witchcraft or contacting the dead."

"I can relate to that."

"But the part that really stayed with me was how she said that witchcraft was all about her trying to control her world. As if she could be the goddess of her own life. But when she came to the end of her rope, she had to admit it was impossible, not to mention frustrating."

I nod. "Yes, I've felt like that too."

"You see, being a Christian is about giving up all that control. It's as if you've been driving for days and you're hopelessly lost and turned around and tired, and so you get out of the driver's seat and simply let God take the wheel. And he makes sure you get home safely. It's about trusting him, the one who put all the stars in place, to chart your course. One of my favorite Scriptures is Proverbs 3:5-6, and it says that we need to trust God with our whole hearts, and that we shouldn't rely on our own insight and understanding but that we should acknowledge God in everything and then he'll show us the best way to go."

"Does that really work?"

"It works for me and every other Christian I know. Certainly, it doesn't mean that life is perfect or smooth or easy-breezy. God plans for us to have bumps along the way. That's what makes us grow, makes us strong, and most importantly, makes us lean on him. God promises to replace our weakness with his strength—as long as we admit our weakness and let him step in and take over."

"I feel pretty weak right now," I admit. "And hopeless and useless and pathetic and flaky and—"

"I get the picture," she says. "And it's good that you can admit those things, Heather, but you don't need to beat yourself up, either. God wants you to confess to him where you've gone wrong, and then he wants you to accept his forgiveness and invite him to come and live inside you."

"That sounds too easy."

"Fortunately, God did keep it fairly simple. Unlike witchcraft, with all its rules and rituals and formulas, Christianity is pretty straightforward. I think God knew that we couldn't handle too much. John 3:16 lays it out pretty clearly by saying that God loved the whole world so much that he gave his only Son, Jesus, so that whoever believed in him could live forever." She smiles at me with kind blue eyes. "That's what your mom did, Heather. And she's with him now."

"You really do believe that."

"Yes, I do. And I believe that's what God wants for you, too."

This is followed by a long moment of silence. And, whether it seems flaky or not, I know what I have to do. "Can you help me to do that?" I ask.

"Do you want to invite Jesus into your heart?"

"Yes, but I really don't know how to pray."

She smiles. "How about if I show you. I'll say a line and you just repeat it after me, okay?"

"Okay."

"Dear heavenly Father," she begins and I echo her words, making them my own. "I believe that you sent your only son Jesus to die in my place . . . so that I might have a personal relationship with you . . . I thank you for your mercy and forgiveness . . . I receive you into my heart right now . . . and I thank you for how much you truly love me . . . I thank you for all that you want to do in my life . . . and I thank you for forgiving me for my involvement in witchcraft . . . please, fill me so full of your spirit that there will never be room for any other spirits . . . thank you for coming into my heart today."

I feel more tears filling my eyes as I say "amen." But this time they are tears of relief. "I don't know if I can explain it," I tell her, "but I know this is real. Not real like I thought witchcraft was real, but real in the sense that I feel different inside. I feel clean and peaceful and . . ." I pause to consider this new sensation. *"Hopeful."*

"And only God can do that," she says.

"What do I do now?" I ask eagerly.

"You do as God leads you."

As it turns out, God leads me to spend the rest of the week with Diane. Of course, she insists that we call my dad first. To my relief, she handles it for me. And I'm not surprised to hear that he doesn't even mind.

"I have a feeling he'd like it if I never came back," I confess to her at dinner that night.

"No, I don't think so," she says slowly. "He sounded genuinely sad. He said that he knows he's been distracted with the Yaquina Lake case. I guess it goes to court next week. That's got to be a lot of pressure for him."

"Yeah. He sort of turned into a workaholic after Mom died. But this case in particular has consumed a lot of his time. I'm really hoping that he wins it. Maybe not so much for his sake, since I guess I'm still pretty mad at him, but for the sake of the lake, I hope he wins."

Diane says we'll call this my spiritual rehabilitation week. And she doesn't even seem too concerned that I'm missing school. "It's better than missing your life," she assures me, and I know she's referring to my unsuccessful suicide plan. "Not that I'm usually supportive of kids cutting school," she continues as we clean up the dinner things. "My two boys both gave that a try, and I set them straight."

"Where are they?" I ask as I rinse a plate.

"Both in college. Aaron graduates this spring. But Tim is just a freshman. It's my first official empty-nester year, which was one reason my sister and I had planned our fall trip."

"So I come along and invade your sweet empty nest."

"And I'm so glad you did, Heather. To be honest, I was feeling a little lonely and blue the day you showed up. I believe that God had a twofold purpose in bringing you here."

"I feel so at home here," I say. I can hear the longing in my voice and know I must sound pathetic. But the thought of returning home to Dad and Augustine, even after a week away, is pretty unnerving. Still, I know that God is supposed to strengthen me. At least that's what Diane keeps saying.

"I wouldn't have a problem with you staying here indefinitely," she says as she puts a glass in the dishwasher. "But I'm not sure that would be best for you. I wouldn't want to tempt you to run away from something you need to face."

"But what if I face it and it blows up in my face?"

"I've considered that possibility, Heather. Whatever happens, I want you to know that you'd be welcome here. But we both need to pray about this; we need to ask God to lead. Okay?"

I nod. "Yeah. That's what I'm trying to do."

I spend the week praying and reading the Bible, talking with Diane, helping around the house, and I've also been doing a lot of sleeping. I think my short stint in witchcraft took a lot out of me and put me in need of a serious rest. But finally it's Sunday, and after going to church with Diane, I know it's time for me to head home.

"Do you have a good home church?" asks Diane's best friend, Barbara Marshall. Barbara knows a little about my situation and is pretty sympathetic.

"I've only gone to church with a friend," I admit. "But to be honest, I never really felt at home there. Her pastor likes to yell a lot and it kind of bugs me. But maybe it'll be different now that I'm a Christian."

Barbara laughs. "I don't know about you, Diane, but I've never liked pastors who yell, and I've been a Christian most of my life."

"I really like your church," I tell them. "I actually felt totally comfortable here. I love how they use things like art and music. It was really beautiful."

"There's a church like that in your town," says Barbara. "I don't recall the name, but a friend of mine goes there. I could write down her name and phone number for you." She digs in her purse for pen and paper, then jots something down and hands it to me.

"Naomi Lamb?" I say suddenly.

"You know her?"

"She's my ballet teacher," I say. "And I really like her. I knew she went to church, but she never really talks about it."

Barbara nods. "That sounds like Naomi. She's always been respectful of personal space, doesn't like to offend. But she is a sweetheart."

"I can't wait to ask her about her church," I say.

And then I am back in my car, driving back down the exact same road that I was on just a week ago. But everything is different. In the same way this car has done a 180 turn, so has my life. I just pray that God gets me through whatever lies ahead. "I feel very weak right now," I admit as I drive. "But Diane said that you can become strong in my weakness, God. Please, make me strong. I surrender it all to you. Help me. Amen."

# twenty

To my surprise, Augustine is not there when I get home. Not there, as in she has left for good, my dad sadly tells me.

"Was it because of me?" I ask.

"No. It was because of me."

"You mean because you really weren't comfortable with the affair?"

His brows draw together. *"The affair?"*

"You know," I remind him. "With Jonathon."

He frowns. "You mean *the kiss?"*

*"The kiss?"*

"Augustine told me how you walked in when Jonathon kissed her."

"What?"

"Last weekend," he says. "Wasn't that what the whole fight between us was about? You blew Jonathon's innocent little kiss all out of proportion, accusing Augustine of all sorts of horrible things."

*"That's* what she told you?"

"Isn't that what happened?"

I just shake my head in wonder. "I can't believe that's what she told you, Dad. That is *not* what happened. Not at all. No wonder it made no sense. I couldn't believe you'd take what they did so lightly."

"You mean the kiss?"

"No, Dad. I do not mean the kiss." Then I tell him about what really happened the day I came home early. And I spare him no details.

"That's the truth?" he asks incredulously.

"I swear that's the truth."

He leans forward and, putting his head between his hands, lets out a low groan.

I go over to where he's sitting on the couch and put a hand on his shoulder. "I'm sorry, Dad. I hate that she's hurt you."

"And then lied about it," he says, looking up with moist eyes. "Her lie drove a wedge between you and me, Heather. I'm sorry I believed her."

I nod, swallowing against the huge lump in my throat. "It hurt a lot when you took her side. I thought you actually felt it was fine for her to sleep with Jonathan and I was so confused. I mean, it just didn't seem right."

"I may be liberal about some things, but not that. I expect fidelity from a wife." He sighs. "And now it all begins to make sense."

"What do you mean?"

"Oh, things she's been saying this past month. About the same time dear Jonathon showed up. It's clear that she was in love with him. I was just too blind to see it."

"I'd seen them together before that day," I admit. "And I guess I was a little suspicious, but I was so distracted by my own messed-up life, well, I just didn't pay much attention." Then I tell Dad about how Augustine was so supportive of me going to the witch seminar.

He nods. "Yes. I wasn't very excited about it myself, but Augustine really pressured me to agree to it. In fact, as I recall, she sort of guilted me into it."

"So that we'd both be gone for a whole weekend," I say. "But I spoiled it by coming home early."

He nods. "And why was that? I never really did hear that part."

So I tell him about it. Then I tell him about what happened while I was at Diane's.

"That Diane," he says, shaking his head. "Talk about a woman of influence."

"But a good influence," I point out.

"I suppose."

"She is, Dad. If you don't watch it, I'll make you go visit her someday."

He sort of laughs. "I'm not ready for that right now, Heather."

"Well, it's just a matter of time," I tell him. "Diane and I are both praying for you."

"Two women of influence?"

I firmly nod.

"Well, there's a pile of homework for you in your room."

"Huh?"

"I called your friend Lucy. And, yes, I know you girls haven't been too friendly lately. But she's a nice girl and she agreed to pick up some things for you."

"Thanks a lot," I say sarcastically, even though I know it was probably a smart thing to do.

"Another thing," he says, reaching for his wallet. Is he about to give me money? "I found this in Augustine's things, but I'm fairly certain it isn't hers." He carefully hands me the old photo of my mom—the one I removed from my locket back when I did that stupid love potion.

I feel tears coming as I study the slightly wrinkled photo. "Thanks, Dad."

"I thought you'd want it back."

I go upstairs and put the photo back into my locket. I'm not sure why Augustine took it, but I'm not that surprised that she did. I don't think she could do much else to surprise me. But even as I think this, I realize that I'm not much different from her. At least I wasn't. Hopefully I'll be changing now that God is at work inside me. As I try to focus on my pile of homework, I remember some things that Diane told me. How I need to get rid of the things related to Wicca and how I'll need to really pray against some spirits and things. I even call Lucy and tell her about my total turnaround.

"Oh, Heather," she says happily. "That's so awesome. I've been praying for you like crazy this past week."

"And I wanted to tell you that I'm really sorry for treating you so badly," I continue. "I was a lousy friend."

"I'm sorry too!" she blurts out. "I know that I was being a pretty poor excuse of a Christian. I told my youth pastor about some of the things I'd said to you a few weeks ago. I was like all proud of myself, thinking I was being such a strong Christian, and he told me that I was totally wrong and that if I wanted to be like Jesus, I would quit judging you and start loving you." She sighs. "But I didn't even listen."

Then I spend the next week making public apologies and eating humble pie as I admit to my friends that I was all wet when it came to Wicca.

"Lucy was so right about Wicca," I confess in front of my old friends at the lunch table on Monday. "It really is witchcraft, and it's very bad. *Very, very bad.*" Then I take my confession another step and tell them about how I found God. Oh, I don't go into all the details just yet—I can save some things for later. But I do tell them that I know this is the real deal. "And, okay, I'm sure everyone thinks I'm totally flaky by now. I mean, first I go vegan and then give it up. Then I go Wiccan and quit that. But at least I'm learning. And I know that God's the real deal, not that I expect you to believe me, but I'm sure that time will prove I'm right."

"Oh, you're right," says Lucy, relief shining in her eyes. "You are *so* right."

"Where's Liz?" I ask.

"Didn't you hear?" says Chelsea.

"What?"

"She went up to St. Anthony's the middle of last week," says Lucy solemnly.

"*St. Anthony's?*" I repeat. I, of all people, am well aware that it's a cancer treatment center. My mom spent a lot of time there before they gave up on her. "Why?"

"We don't know for sure," says Chelsea. "Even Hudson is in the dark. They broke up, by the way."

"But is Liz okay?" My voice breaks as I ask this. All I can think of is the horrible curse that I tried to put on her. Although I thought that it had only backfired, coming back at me with three times the evil I intended for her. I guess I assumed that meant it hadn't worked on her. Now I'm not so sure. And I'm feeling pretty scared for her, and guilty!

"We're praying for her," says Lucy. "It must be serious."

"I'll pray for her too," I say. And I will. I will pray night and day. I will beg the God who is bigger than witchcraft to spare her from anything I might've created. I even confess my stupidity to Lucy, and as soon as school's over we go back to the beach where I buried that moronic witch's bottle. But we dig and dig and never find it. Finally, Lucy tells me that God is bigger than any magic I tried to create, and we both get down on our knees and ask God to replace my bad intentions with his healing powers. I hug Lucy and thank her for being my friend. Then she comes home with me and prays over my room. I've already disposed of all my lame witch's junk. Talk about some expensive lessons.

Then on Tuesday, right before ballet, I ask Naomi about Liz. She's Liz's godmother; she should know something. I can feel Sienna watching me from where she's seated at the piano. I have no idea what she's thinking. And I don't really care at the moment. All I care about is Liz and whether I've brought harm onto her.

"Haven't you heard?" asks Naomi.

I shake my head, waiting for the ground to drop away from under me when I learn the horrible news. Please, God, please let Liz be okay.

"She's perfectly fine," says Naomi with a smile. "Her mom called me last night."

"But why was she at the cancer center?" I ask.

She frowns. "Liz didn't tell you?"

"What?"

"She didn't mention that she had leukemia as a child? And that every year they do a full spectrum of tests on her just to make sure she's still in remission?"

"No, she didn't tell me."

"And she is!"

I hug Naomi. "Thank God!"

"And there she is now," she says, nodding to the door that Liz is just coming through.

I run over and hug Liz now. I tell her I'm sorry that I acted like such a horrible person and I ask her to forgive me.

"Of course," she says, laughing. "No hard feelings."

"And now that I finally have you both here in the same room," Naomi adds, "I want to ask you something."

"Go for it," asks Liz.

"I want to know if you'd be willing to share the part of the Sugar Plum Fairy in this year's Christmas performance."

"Share it?" says Liz. "How do you do that?"

"I'm not completely sure," she admits. "I thought if you both learned it, you could either take turns, since there will be four performances. Or perhaps, if we could make it look right, you could dance a duet. I'm not sure, but we can figure it out. Are you willing?"

"Sure," I tell her. "I figured Liz was going to get that part anyway."

Naomi frowns. "But you knew it was your year, Heather, didn't you?"

I shrug. "To be honest, I've had my head in a hole since last summer. I've just started to see the light."

"Cool," says Liz. "Now maybe you can show me how to find it."

I laugh. "Actually, I'm not much of an expert. In fact, I was about to ask Naomi about visiting her church. Maybe you should come too."

Then Naomi claps her hands. "Time to dance." But she nods at me. "We'll discuss that later."

As we dance, I see Sienna peering curiously at me, and I realize that I'm going to have to explain everything to her. And, actually, I think I'm looking forward to it. But first I'll have to start praying for her. Because, despite everything, I think that God wants me to reach out to this woman, and I know that he loves her as much as he loves me. I just hope that she'll be able to receive that love.

After class, Liz and I go to the WC for coffee, and I tell her a little more about all that's gone on in my life these past few weeks. I even confess to her about the charm I put in her car.

"Was that what that was?" She throws her head back and laughs. "I'd been smelling something rancid in there, and I looked around and found this stinking bag. I thought it was some kind of rotten food that I'd forgotten about. I threw it out and got my car cleaned too."

"Good." I shake my head. "And I'm so sorry."

She just waves her hand. "No problem. So tell me, have you really given up this Wicca biz for good then? No stirring a big black caldron or riding your broomstick around on Halloween next week?"

I laugh. "Hey, I noticed that Halloween is on Sunday this year, which means you'll probably find this girl in church."

As I'm driving home, it occurs to me that many of my recent problems seem to have evaporated. Oh, not everything, of course. I mean there's still the Yaquina Lake dispute to be settled, although it's looking a tiny bit better. Then there's my poor old dad's broken heart, but he has hired a decorator to redo our house according to our tastes, and I think that's a healthy step. And, as far as I go, I know for a fact that I'll never get Hudson back, but I'm dealing with that. But, really, a whole lot of other troublesome things seem to have simply vanished—just like magic.

*No,* I correct myself as I turn into my driveway, *just like God!*

# reader's guide

1. What did Heather want for her life that she thought Wicca could provide?

2. Why do you think Wicca can be initially attractive to those who are seeking spiritual answers?

3. Think about the women Heather meets who practice Wicca—Willow, Sienna, Jane, Marie. How do they compare to your idea of witches? Did anything about them surprise you?

4. Describe the kind of people you think are most susceptible to the influence of Wicca and witchcraft. Why do you think that is?

5. Why do you think the witches in this story could not control whether the spiritual forces in their lives were good or evil?

6. What are some of the ways you try to get control of the circumstances in your life? What do you imagine God thinks about those methods?

7. What part of Heather's story was most frightening to you? Why?

8. Why do you think the Bible has such strong admonitions against practicing witchcraft? (See, for example, Deuteronomy 18; 1 Samuel 28 and 31.)

9. If you were Heather's best friend, how would you advise her concerning her involvement in witchcraft?

10. Practitioners of witchcraft believe that they are the goddess or god of their own lives and that they are in control of all that happens. Who is god of your life? What controls you?

# TrueColors Book 12

# Harsh Pink

## Coming in June 2007

Sometimes the need to survive justifies the means.

## One

A PRETTY BLONDE GIRL SAUNTERS OVER TO WHERE I'M SEATED ON A CEMENT bench in the courtyard. It's a warm September day and I've been reading a book and basically minding my own business, waiting for the lunch break to end so I can go to class. I continue looking down at my book, pretending I haven't noticed this girl, pretending like I couldn't care less that she's staring at me. I don't actually *know* this girl, although I've seen her around. And I definitely know her type. In some ways I *am* her type. For starters, she's the kind of girl who wears the right designer and wears it well. Not in the flashy, overdone, Paris Hilton sort of way, but in a way that shows she has a good sense of style and class. She keeps her makeup impeccable without looking cheap, and her highlights appear totally natural. She's looking at me with an expression of superiority mixed with boredom, as if I'm not really worthy of her attention, but for some reason she has set her sights on me. She places one hand on her hip, striking a pose I'm sure for the benefit of her friends, who are packed together, whispering, about twenty feet away. Her upper lip curls ever so slightly, as if she's just gotten a whiff of something that smells bad. And then she speaks. "So *you're* the one."

I close my paperback and study her carefully, taking my time to respond, waiting just long enough to make her a little uneasy, or so I hope. "The one *what*?" I keep my tone even. No way do I want her to know she's making me uncomfortable. The first step toward losing power is to let them see you squirm. I know this because I know how to make others squirm. Sometimes it's necessary.

"The one who *somehow* made it onto the varsity cheerleading squad." Now she's actually looking down her nose at me. And that's when I notice that there's a slight ball on the tip of her nose and, from my angle, it's just a bit reminiscent of Miss Piggy. Enough that it makes me actually smile. So she's not so perfect after all.

"What's so funny?"

I just shrug as I slip my book into the oversized Burberry bag that I snagged from my mom's closet last weekend. "I assume you stopped by to offer me your hearty congratulations." I make sure she can hear the sarcasm in my voice, then I slowly stand. Of course, I wonder why I bother, since she's at least six inches taller than me and I'm still looking up at her. My five-foot stature has some perks, like when it comes to gymnastics or being tossed high in an exuberant cheerleading stunt, but it gives me a definite disadvantage in power struggles like this.

"Who *are* you anyway?" she asks as if she's the reigning queen of Belmont High. Maybe she is.

"Reagan Mercer," I say lightly. "Pleased to make your acquaintance, uh, whoever *you* are."

"Everyone *knows* who I am," she nods toward her friends, who are slowly meandering over as if on cue. Now I notice that they are some of the same girls who tried out yesterday. "I'm Kendra Farnsworth," she continues in that smug, superior tone, "the girl that you *barely* beat out for varsity squad. In fact, I'm first alternate, not that I care." She looks as if she's about to yawn now. Perhaps she's boring herself as much as she's boring me. But she's not finished. "I've been cheering since middle school and I was on varsity last year, and if you hadn't dropped in, like out of nowhere, well, I'd still be on varsity right now. Not that I care so much, since I think I've outgrown that whole scene."

Suddenly I remember this girl with clarity. As usual, I had tried not to watch as the other girls did their routines during tryouts yesterday. It's just my way. I figure if they do really well, I'll get discouraged and lose my competitive edge. Or if they totally flop, I'll get overconfident and not give it my best shot. For me, it's just better not to watch. But suddenly I remember this girl and exactly what went wrong. She started out just fine, but then she forgot the second half of the long routine. Oh, she did it with a fair amount of grace and style and actually laughed at herself, then did a couple of really good jumps that made the crowd cheer. Still, to forget that much of the routine . . . well, it didn't look too promising to me. And apparently it had cost her a position on the squad. Like that's my fault.

The list was only posted this morning, and since the other names are still unfamiliar to me, I only looked at it to make sure my name was on it. Even then I contained my enthusiasm, covered my pleased surprise. Because despite knowing I'd performed a flawless routine and even thrown in a couple of backflips that seemed to impress the crowd, you can never be sure. So when I read my name on the list today, I just sort of nodded, did a silent internal cheer, then went on my way. I'm fully aware that I need to play this out carefully. Being the new girl comes with all kinds of challenges and liabilities. Obviously Kendra Farnsworth is one of them.

"Sorry about that," I say in a voice that I mean to sound genuine. "That's a tough break."

She rolls her eyes, then studies a perfectly shaped fingernail. "Tell me about it."

I look at her French manicure with those white tips that never look real. I'm surprised she hasn't heard that French is out, but maybe she doesn't care. "I forgot part of a routine once," I say offhandedly. "It was in a state competition." Okay, that is a total lie, but I need to get her to trust me by appearing to be transparent. The truth is I was really worried that I'd forget our hardest routine when we competed at state last year, but it never actually happened. I made sure it didn't. But my "confession" does the trick. It causes Kendra to smile, ever so slightly, and I think maybe the ice is thawing a little. She gives a nod over to where her friends are standing and, as if on cue, they come over and begin talking to me, introducing themselves and cautiously congratulating me for making the squad. Apparently some of them made it too.

"Where are you *from* anyway?" asks a petite brunette named Sally.

Now, this is one of those questions that can easily be taken wrong. Sometimes people ask me where I'm from, as in, "What's your ethnic background?" Because of my Asian features, some people have even assumed I can't speak English—which can be either amusing or irritating, depending on my mood. But, under these circumstances, I decide to give Sally the benefit of the doubt.

"We moved here from Boston last summer," I explain. "I'd been a cheerleader at my old high school since freshman year." This I say for Kendra's benefit, although my eyes are still on Sally. "And I cheered in middle school before that." I shrug. "Between gymnastics and cheerleading, it seems like I've spent most of my life bouncing around." I sort of laugh.

"Well, you were really good yesterday," says a skinny blonde as she pokes Kendra in the arm. "I mean, you totally rocked Kendra's world."

"Shut *up*, Meredith," snaps Kendra.

"Hey, it's your own dumb fault," says Meredith. "We told you to practice, but you were like all, 'No, I don't need to.'"

"Whatever." Kendra narrows her eyes and adjusts the strap of her Fendi bag. "Like I told Reagan, I've decided that cheering is juvenile anyway. This is my senior year and I've got better things to do."

"Yeah, like what?" challenges Meredith.

"Like Logan Worthington," Kendra says with a sly expression. "I wouldn't mind doing that boy this year."

Sally laughs. "He's about the only one you haven't done."

"What is this?" says Kendra with a wounded expression. "Bash Kendra Day? Isn't it bad enough that I didn't make the squad, but all my friends have to turn on me too?"

Of course, this plea for mercy changes everything. And suddenly these girls are apologizing, offering condolences, and practically offering to carry her books. Not that she has any. Kendra just smiles, a glimmer of triumph in her eyes. "That's better." Then it's time to head back to class.

"Nice meeting you guys," I say as I head off toward the English department. They call out similar pleasantries, but I can tell that this isn't over. I know enough about girls to know that it's never really over. And I suspect Kendra isn't ready to let this go yet. The question is, how far will she take it?

It's times like this when you need a good friend by your side. I remember my best friend, Geneva, back in Boston. Man, do I wish she were here now. Not only was Geneva gorgeous and intelligent and lots of fun, but she could easily hold her own against girls like Kendra. Geneva and I made a pretty daunting pair. I doubt that I'll ever have anyone quite like her again. That makes me sad. Good friends aren't easy to come by.

I've developed my own classification system when it comes to friends. I rank them as A, B, or C. Naturally, Geneva was an A. Actually, she was an A-plus. My second best friend, Bethany, was a B, but she was better than nothing if Geneva was unavailable. C friends are more a matter of desperate convenience. Like if you're late to lunch and have to stand in the line by yourself, to keep from looking pathetic you talk to someone that you'd normally just ignore.

Then we moved here last summer, and now I have to start over. I don't even have a C friend. Oh, I hung with one for a few weeks. My grandma introduced me to a neighbor girl and, for Nana's sake, I tried to be nice to this somewhat lame girl. Although it did worry me that someone might see me with her and I'd be classified even before school started. Fortunately, that didn't seem to happen. But the sad truth was that poor Andrea Lynch was definitely a C friend—more like a C-minus. To be fair, she might've made it to a plus if I'd stuck with her.

After a couple of weeks, I'd trained her to quit laughing through her nose, which was totally gross sounding, and her complexion actually started to clear up after I introduced her to a proper skin-care regime. And I have to admit that she did have this quirky sense of humor and we even had some good laughs. But a few days before school started, I dumped Andrea so fast that I'm sure her head is still spinning. I've been utilizing my caller ID to avoid taking her phone calls, and I even went so far as to block her e-mails. We're talking cold turkey here. I'm fully aware that was pretty heartless on my part. But when you're the new girl in town, you have to fend for yourself. And I'm smart enough to know that friends like Andrea Lynch are not an asset.

Even when I saw Andrea in school during those first few days, less than a week ago, I pretended not to know her. And I actually ignored her when she called out my name a couple of times, playing blind, deaf, and dumb. The only alternative would've been to set her straight—and that's pretty harsh. Anyway, I think she got the hint. Does that make me a mean girl? No, I reassure myself as I walk into my lit class, taking a seat in the second row. It simply means I'm a survivor.

# about the author

MELODY CARLSON has written over a hundred books for all age groups, but she particularly enjoys writing for teens. Perhaps this is because her own teen years remain so vivid in her memory. After claiming to be an atheist at the ripe old age of twelve, she later surrendered her heart to Jesus and has been following him ever since. Her hope and prayer for all her readers is that each one would be touched by God in a special way through her stories. For more information, please visit Melody's website at www.melodycarlson.com.

## Pitch Black: Color Me Lost

Morgan Bergstrom thinks her life is as bad as it can get, but it's about to get a whole lot worse. Her close friend Jason Harding has just killed himself, and no one knows why. As she struggles with her grief, Morgan must make her life's ultimate decision — before it's too late.
1-57683-532-4

## Burnt Orange: Color Me Wasted

Amber Conrad has a problem: Her youth group friends Simi and Lisa won't get off her case about the drinking parties she's been going to. Everyone does it. What's the big deal? Will she be honest with herself and her friends before things really get out of control?
1-57683-533-2

## Fool's Gold: Color Me Consumed

On furlough from Papua New Guinea, Hannah Johnson spends some time with her Prada-wearing cousin, Vanessa. Hannah feels like an alien around her host — everything Vanessa has is so nice. Hannah knows that stuff's not supposed to matter, but why does she feel a twinge of jealousy deep down inside?
1-57683-534-0

## Blade Silver: Color Me Scarred

As Ruth Wallace attempts to stop cutting, her family life deteriorates further to the point that she isn't sure she'll ever be able to stop. Ruth needs help, but will she get it before this habit threatens her life?
1-57683-535-9

## Bitter Rose: Color Me Crushed

Maggie's parents suddenly split up after twenty-five years of marriage. The whole situation has Maggie feeling hurt, distraught, and, most of all, violently bitter. She's near desperate for someone who can restore her confidence in love.
1-57683-536-7

## Faded Denim: Color Me Trapped

Emily hates her overweight body, her insecure personality, and sometimes even her "perfect" friends. She takes drastic measures to change her body, but the real issues are weighing down her heavy heart.
1-57683-537-5

## Bright Purple: Color Me Confused

Ramie Grant cannot believe it when her best friend, Jessica, tells her she's a homosexual. It's just a matter of time before others on the basketball team find out. Quickly, little jokes become vicious attacks. In the end, Ramie must decide if she will stand by Jessica's side or turn her back on a friend in need.
1-57683-950-8

# Diaries Are a Girl's Best Friend